THE
INVENTION
OF
HUGO
CABRET

THE
INVENTION
OF
HUGO
CABRET

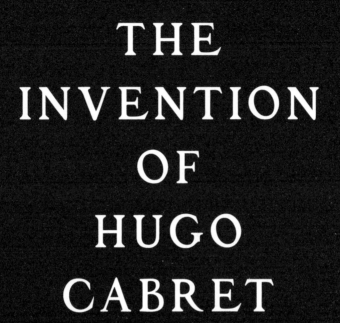

A Novel in Words and Pictures

by Brian Selznick

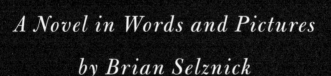

Scholastic Press · New York

All rights reserved. Published by Scholastic Press, an imprint of Scholastic Inc.,
Publishers since 1920. SCHOLASTIC, SCHOLASTIC PRESS, and associated
logos are trademarks and/or registered trademarks of Scholastic Inc.

LIBRARY OF CONGRESS CATALOGING-IN-PUBLICATION DATA
Selznick, Brian.
The invention of Hugo Cabret / by Brian Selznick. — 1st ed. p. cm.
Summary: When twelve-year-old Hugo, an orphan living and repairing clocks
within the walls of a Paris train station in 1931, meets a mysterious toyseller and his
goddaughter, his undercover life and his biggest secret are jeopardized.
ISBN-13 : 978-0-439-81378-5   ISBN-10 : 0-439-81378-6 (hardcover)
1. Méliès, Georges, 1861-1938—Juvenile fiction. [1. Méliès, Georges, 1861-
1938—Fiction. 2. Robots—Fiction. 3. Orphans—Fiction. 4. Railroad
stations—Fiction. 5. Paris (France)—History—1870-1940—Fiction.
6. France—History—Third Republic, 1870-1940—Fiction.] I. Title.
PZ7.S4654Inv 2007   [Fic]—dc22   2006007119

10   9   8   7   6   15   16   17   18   19

Printed in the U.S.A.   23
First edition, March 2007

Book design by David Saylor, Charles Kreloff, and Brian Selznick

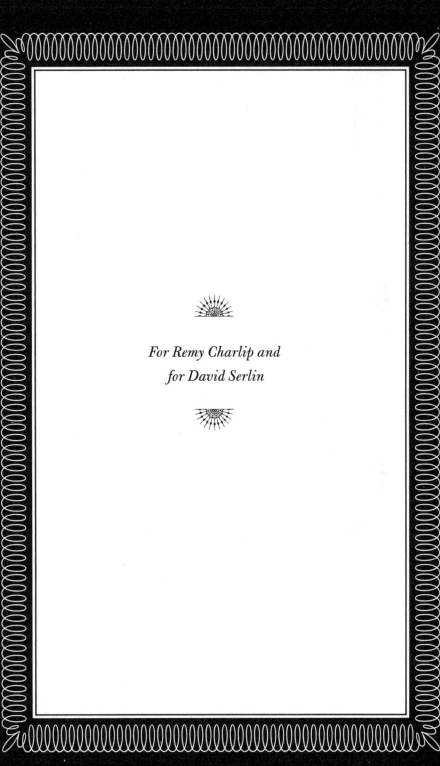

For Remy Charlip and
for David Serlin

CONTENTS

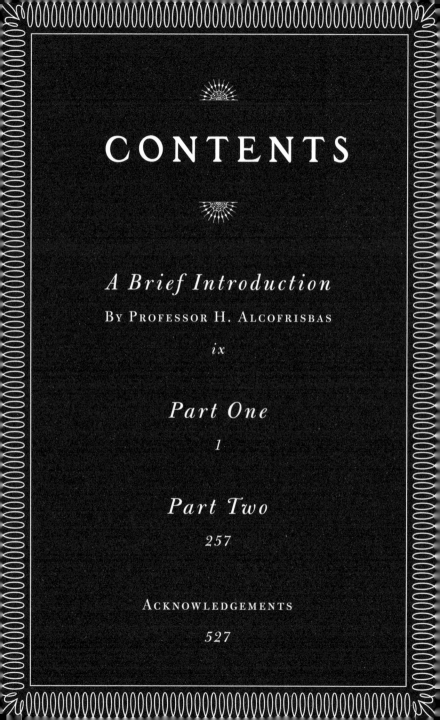

A BRIEF
INTRODUCTION

THE STORY I AM ABOUT TO SHARE with you takes place in 1931, under the roofs of Paris. Here you will meet a boy named Hugo Cabret, who once, long ago, discovered a mysterious drawing that changed his life forever.

But before you turn the page, I want you to picture yourself sitting in the darkness, like the beginning of a movie. On screen, the sun will soon rise, and you will find yourself zooming toward a train station in the middle of the city. You will rush through the doors into a crowded lobby. You will eventually spot a boy amid the crowd, and he will start to move through the train station. Follow him, because this is Hugo Cabret. His head is full of secrets, and he's waiting for his story to begin.

— Professor H. Alcofrisbas

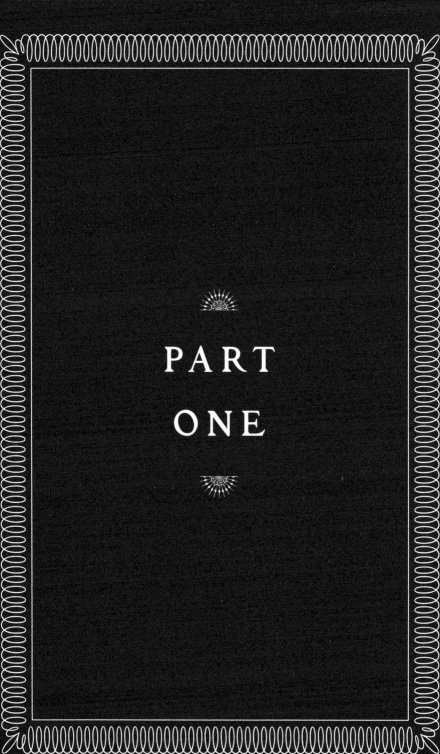

PART
ONE

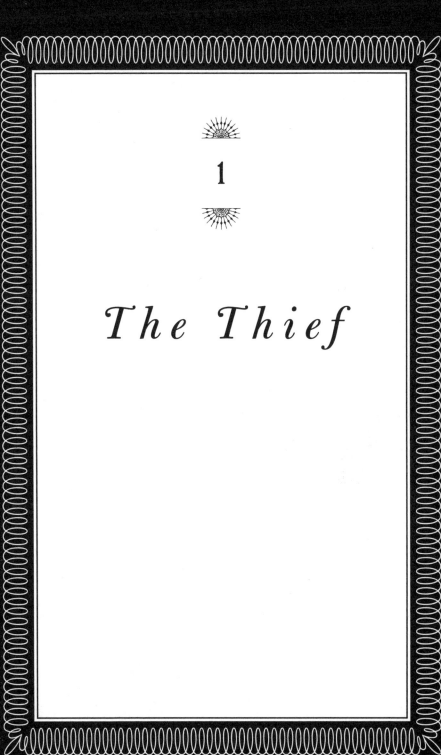

1

The Thief

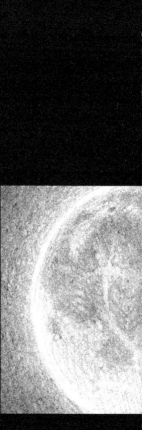

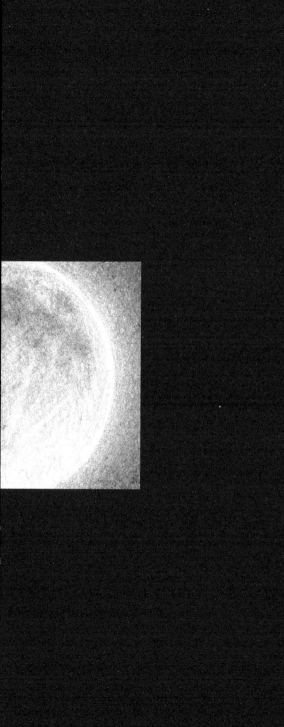

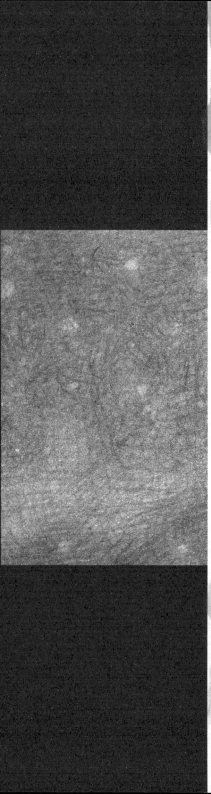

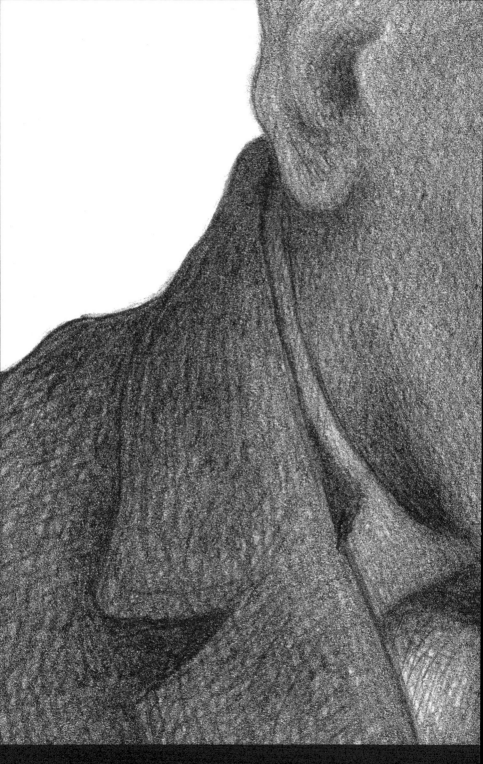

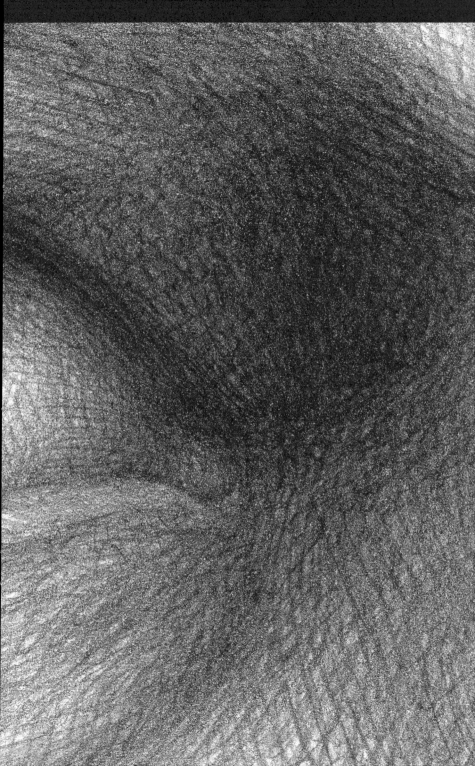

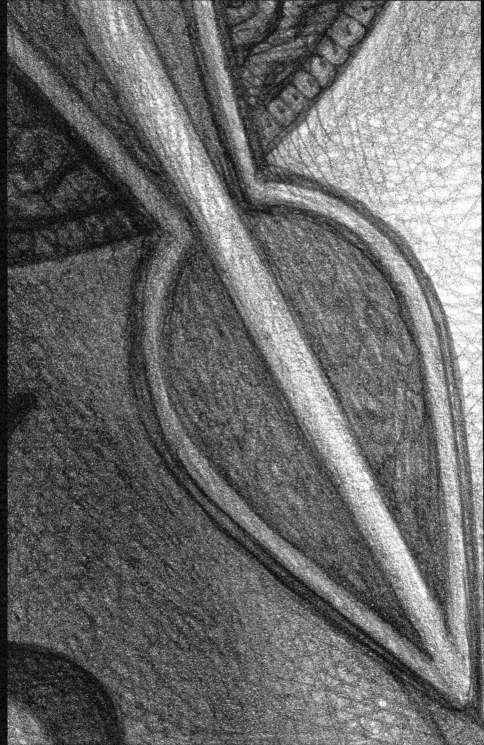

From his perch behind the clock, Hugo could see everything. He rubbed his fingers nervously against the small notebook in his pocket and told himself to be patient.

The old man in the toy booth was arguing with the girl. She was about Hugo's age, and he often saw her go into the booth with a book under her arm and disappear behind the counter.

The old man looked agitated today. Had he figured out some of his toys were missing? Well, there was nothing to be done about that now.

Hugo needed the toys.

The old man and the girl argued some more, and finally she closed her book and ran off.

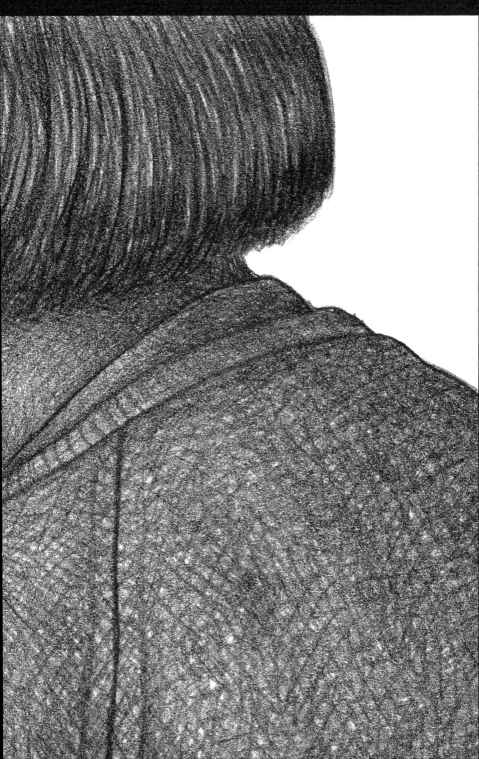

Thankfully, within moments the old man had crossed his arms in front of him and closed his eyes.

Hugo crept through the walls, came out through an air vent, and hurried down the hall until he reached the toy booth. Nervously, he rubbed the notebook one last time, then cautiously lowered his hand around the windup toy he wanted.

But suddenly there was a movement from inside the booth, and the sleeping old man sprang to life. Before Hugo could run, the old man grabbed his arm.

The little blue windup mouse Hugo had taken fell from his hand, skidded across the counter, and landed on the floor with a crack.

"Thief! Thief!" the old man yelled down the empty hallway. "Someone call the Station Inspector!"

At the mention of the Station Inspector, Hugo panicked. He twisted and tried to get away, but the old man pulled hard on his arm and wouldn't let go.

"I finally caught you. Now empty your pockets."

Hugo growled like a dog. He was furious with himself for being caught.

The old man squeezed tighter until Hugo was practically standing on his toes.

"You're hurting me!"

"Empty your pockets!"

Reluctantly, one by one, Hugo pulled out dozens of objects: screws and nails and bits of metal, gears and crumpled playing cards, tiny pieces of clockworks, cogs, and wheels. He pulled out a crushed box of matches and some small candles.

"You have one more pocket to go. . . ." the old man said.

"There's nothing in it."

"Then turn it inside out."

"I don't have anything of yours. Let me go."

"Where is the Station Inspector?" the old man yelled down the hallway again. "Why is he never around when he is needed?"

If the Station Inspector, in his green uniform, appeared at the end of the hallway, Hugo knew everything would be over. The boy struggled against the old man, but it was no use. Finally, his hand trembling, Hugo reached into his pocket and pulled out his small, battered cardboard notebook. The cover had been rubbed smooth.

Still holding on to the boy's arm, the old man snatched the notebook away, set it down out of Hugo's reach, opened it, and flipped through the pages. One page caught the old man's eye.

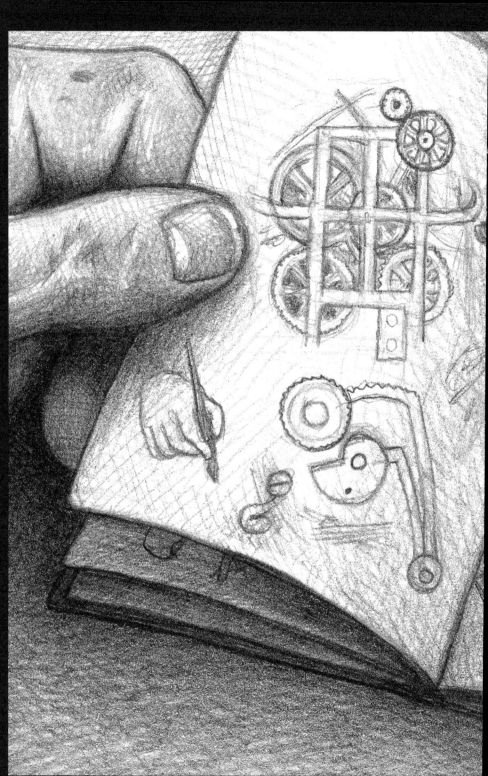

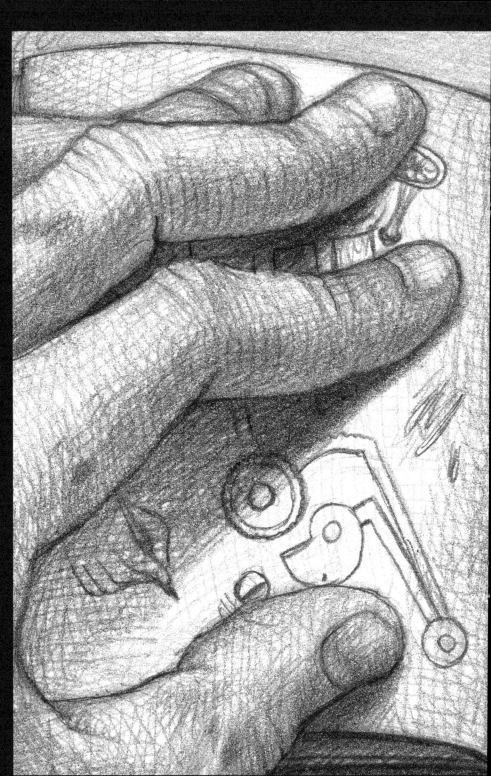

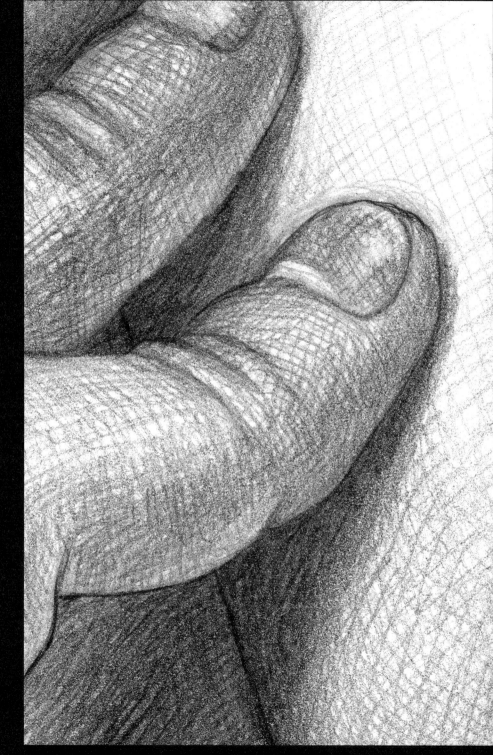

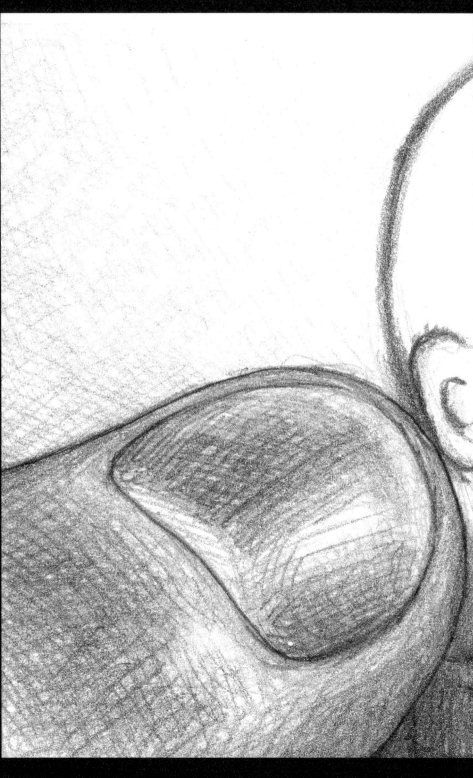

"Give that back to me! It's mine!" cried Hugo.

"Ghosts . . ." the old man muttered to himself. "I knew they would find me here eventually." He closed the notebook. The expression on his face changed rapidly, from fear to sadness to anger. "Who are you, boy? Did you draw these pictures?"

Hugo didn't answer him.

"I said, *did you draw these pictures?*"

Hugo growled again and spit on the floor.

"Who did you steal this notebook from?"

"I didn't steal it."

The old man grunted and with a push he finally let go of Hugo's arm. "Leave me alone, then! Stay away from me and my toy booth."

Hugo rubbed his arm and stepped backward, accidentally crushing the windup mouse he had dropped.

The old man shuddered at the sound of the breaking toy.

Hugo picked up the broken pieces and placed them on the counter. "I can't leave without my notebook."

"It is no longer *your* notebook. It is mine, and I will do with it what I want." The old man waved Hugo's box of matches in the air. "Perhaps I will burn it!"

"No!"

The old man collected the contents of Hugo's

pockets, including the notebook. He placed them in a handkerchief, tied it up, and covered it with his hands. "Then tell me about the drawings. Who did them?"

Hugo said nothing.

The old man slammed a fist down on the counter, shaking all the toys. "Get out of here, you little thief!"

"*You're* the thief!" Hugo yelled as he turned and ran off.

The old man yelled something after him, but all Hugo heard was the clicking of his own shoes echoing off the station walls.

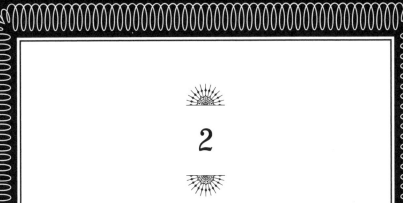

2

The Clocks

HUGO RAN DOWN THE HALLWAY and disappeared back inside the metal vent in the wall. He paused for a moment. The air was cool and damp. A few dim light-bulbs provided a tiny bit of illumination inside the dark passageways.

Hugo opened the door and let himself inside.

Above the ceiling of the main waiting area was a cluster of secret apartments that had been built for the people who ran the train station years ago. Most of them had long been abandoned. Only one was still in use.

Some sunlight filtered through the dirty skylight. Hugo looked at the rows and rows of jars, filled with pieces from all the toys he had stolen from the toy booth over the past few months. The jars sat on shelves made from scavenged planks he had found inside the walls of the station. Under his rickety bed lay a pile of Hugo's drawings. His deck of cards rested on a dusty trunk in the middle of the room. Nearby, on a small table, was a stack of envelopes—his uncle's uncashed paychecks, accumulating week by week.

Hugo wiped his eyes and picked up his bucket of tools. He stuffed some more matches and candles into his pockets and set to work.

As usual, Hugo headed first to the big glass clocks on the roof, because they were the hardest to reach. They were like huge round windows and looked out over the city, one facing north and one facing south. Hugo had to climb up a long dark staircase and slither through an opening in the ceiling at the top of a ladder to get inside them. During the day, his eyes always stung for a few moments from the flood of light through the glass. The motors and gears of these clocks were the biggest in the station, and Hugo was often afraid that his hand was going to get caught.

In the corner of the room, attached by ropes, hung huge weights that kept the clocks running. He checked the time on the glass clocks against the time on his uncle's railroad watch, which he kept with his tools and wound diligently every morning. He then took a moment to carefully look the whole mechanism over, and added a few drops of oil to each gear shaft from a little oilcan in his kit. Hugo's head tilted slightly to the side as he listened to the beat of the clock, waiting until he was sure the machine was running correctly.

Once he had finished with the clocks on the roof, he climbed down the ladder and the long staircase. Back inside the dark passageways, he checked the other clocks in the station, all of which were made of brass and could be maintained from inside the walls.

Hugo lit his candles to help him see and began with the clock that overlooked the ticket booths. This clock, like all the others, had weights, too, but much smaller ones, which disappeared into the floor.

Hugo attached a crank to the back of the clock and, using all of his strength, turned it as far as it would go.

Hugo then made sure the gears and levers were moving accurately, and he checked that the time was correct on the miniature dial built into the back of the clockworks. Next he moved through the hidden passageways to the ring of clocks around the train platforms, and then to the backs of the smaller clocks that faced the interior offices, including the Station Inspector's. Looking through the numbers, Hugo could see the Station Inspector's desk, and in the corner of the office, the cage of a small jail cell that sat waiting for any criminals caught in the station. Hugo had seen men and women locked up in there, and a few times he had even seen boys no older than himself in the cell, their eyes red from crying. Eventually, these people were taken away, and Hugo never saw them again.

From the offices, Hugo followed a long, hidden tunnel to the back of the clock opposite the old man's toy booth. He wished he could avoid this clock, but he knew he couldn't skip any of them. Peering out through the numbers, Hugo spied the old man again, alone in his toy booth at the end of the hallway, looking through the pages of Hugo's notebook. Hugo wanted to scream out, but he didn't. He oiled the clock and listened to it carefully. He could tell it wouldn't need to be wound for another day or two, so Hugo kept going, until all twenty-seven clocks in the station had been attended to, just the way his uncle had taught him.

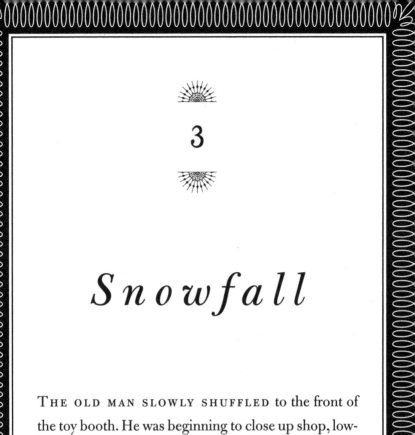

3

Snowfall

THE OLD MAN SLOWLY SHUFFLED to the front of the toy booth. He was beginning to close up shop, lowering the front wooden grate, when Hugo approached him from behind. Hugo knew how to walk silently, but he let his feet fall loudly on the tiles to let the old man know he was there.

"Pick up your feet, boy." The old man glanced over his shoulder. "I hate the sound of shoe heels clicking on the floor." The old man continued to close the grate and lock it.

The halls of the station were nearly empty. Hugo

knew the Station Inspector would be making his evening rounds at the other end of the station, and Hugo figured he had a few minutes before he showed up here.

The old man finished closing up and double-checked the lock on his booth.

"What is your name, boy?"

Hugo hesitated. He was going to lie, but then for some reason he said his real name. "Hugo . . . Hugo Cabret."

"Listen to me, Hugo Cabret. I told you to stay away from me. I will drag you to the Station Inspector's office and lock you up myself if I see you again. Do you understand what I am saying?"

"Give me back my notebook. . . ."

"I am going home to *burn* your notebook."

With that, the old man glanced quickly at the clock across from the toy booth and headed out under the great iron ribs of the train station. He emerged through the golden doors into the dark streets of Paris. It was the end of winter, and a light snow had begun to fall. Hugo watched him go.

It had been a very long time since Hugo had left the train station, and he wasn't dressed for winter, but within moments he burst through the doors.

"You can't burn my notebook!" he shouted to the old man.

"I can," came the answer.

Hugo wanted to tackle him, to knock him to the ground and take back his notebook, but he didn't think he was big enough. And besides, the old man was strong. Hugo's arm still ached from where he had been grabbed earlier.

"Stop clicking the street with your heels," the old man hissed through his teeth. "And don't make me say it again." He shook his head and adjusted his hat. Then, quietly, he said to himself, "I hope the snow covers everything so all the footsteps are silenced, and the whole city can be at peace."

They soon arrived at a decrepit apartment building across from the graveyard. The whole building seemed to lean slightly to the side. Ivy had once covered the walls, but it had been torn away, leaving long interlocking scars in the cracked paint. The old man opened the chipped green door with a large key. Turning back to

Hugo, he said, "Don't you know that the sound of clicking boot heels can summon ghosts? Do you want to be followed by ghosts?"

The old man stepped quickly inside and slammed the door behind him.

4

The Window

HUGO STOOD IN THE DARK OUTSIDE the old man's apartment building. He wiped the snowflakes from his eyelashes and fiddled with the dirty buttons on the front of his thin jacket, rubbing them between his fingers the way he had rubbed the cover of his notebook.

Hugo picked up a stone from the street and threw it at one of the windows, making a loud *clink*.

The curtains parted. A girl looked out. Hugo thought for a second that he had hit the wrong window, but then he recognized the girl.

It was the girl from the toy booth. Hugo was about to yell to her, but she put a finger to her lips and motioned for him to wait there. The curtains closed again.

Hugo shivered in the cold, and in a few minutes the girl appeared from behind the building and ran over to him.

"Who are you?" she asked.

"Your grandfather stole my notebook. I have to get it back before he burns it."

"Papa Georges isn't my grandfather," said the girl. "And he isn't a thief. You are."

"No, I'm not!"

"I saw you."

"How could you have seen me? The old man sent you away before I came to the booth."

"So you were spying on me, too. Well, then we're even."

Hugo looked at the girl curiously. "Let me inside."

"I can't do that. You have to leave."

"I won't go until I have my notebook." Hugo picked up another stone to throw at the window, but the girl grabbed his hand and wrestled the stone from his fingers. She was a little bigger than he was.

"Are you crazy?" she whispered. "I can't get caught out here with you. Why do you need your notebook back so badly?"

"I can't tell you."

Hugo tried to pick up another stone, but the girl pushed him to the ground and held him there. "Listen to me, I can't let you into the building, but I promise I'll make sure he doesn't burn your notebook. Go back to the toy booth tomorrow and ask him for your notebook again."

Hugo looked up into the girl's big dark eyes and realized that he didn't have a choice. She let him stand up, and he ran off into the snowy night.

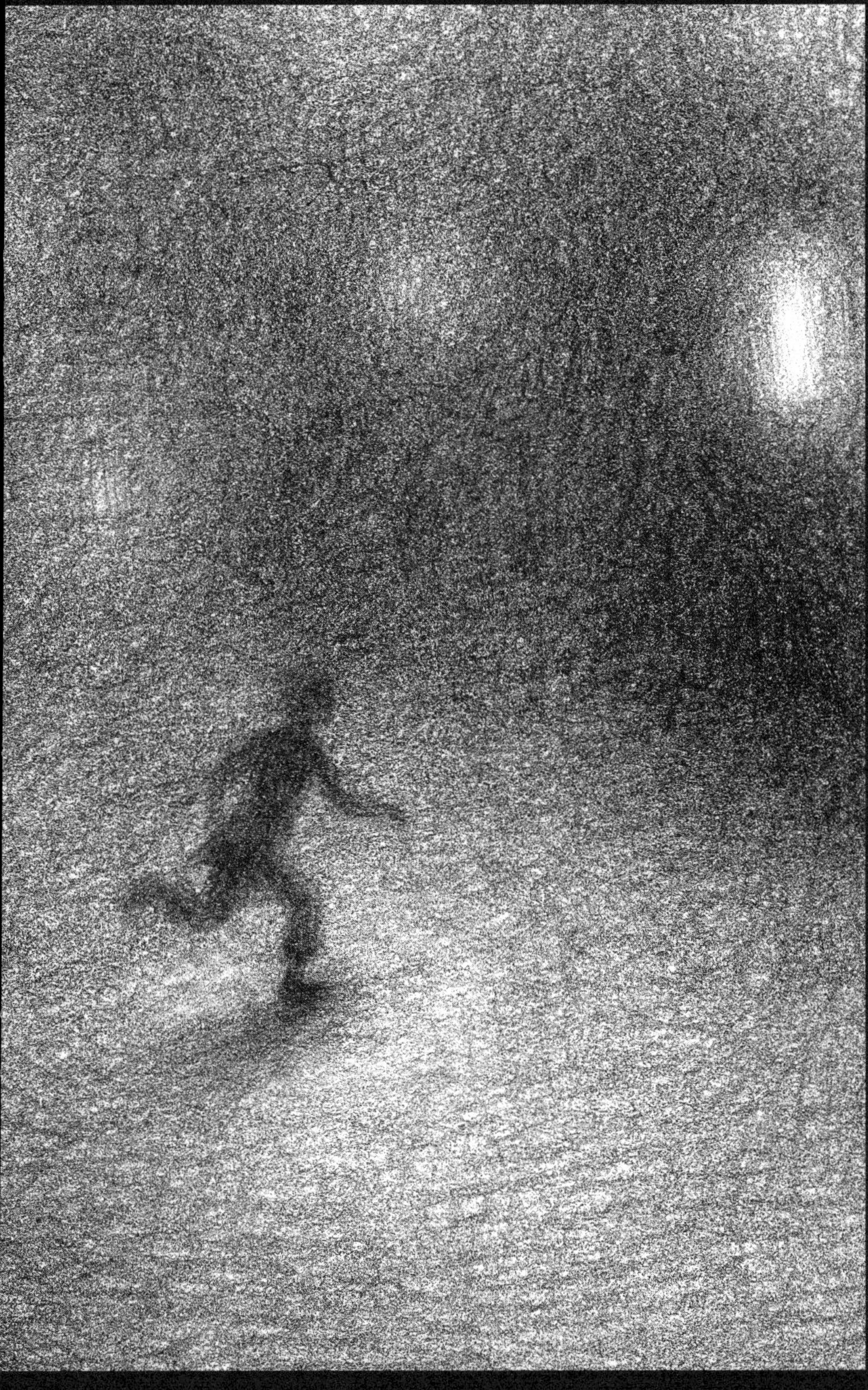

5

Hugo's Father

HUGO RAN UNTIL HE FOUND HIMSELF back inside his secret room. He tried to turn on the light, forgetting, as he usually did, that the bulb in the ceiling had burned out. He struck a match, watched it flare, and lit a few candles. The room filled with a warm golden glow, and huge shadows rose against the walls.

Instinctively, Hugo's fingers reached for the empty pocket where his notebook had been. Not knowing what else to do, he walked to a cluttered pile of boxes in the corner of his room and moved them to the side, revealing a hiding place in the wall.

Hugo reached in and pulled out a large, heavy object.

He untied the frayed ropes and unwrapped the fabric that covered it.

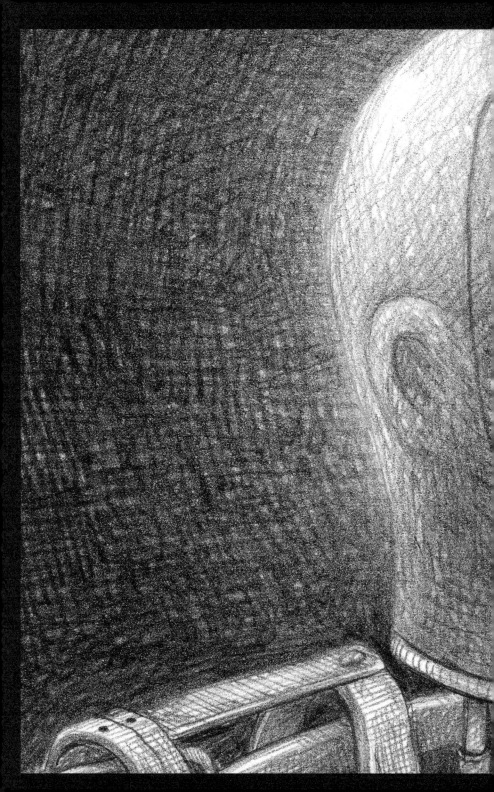

The man was built entirely out of clockworks and fine machinery. From the very first moment his father had told him about it, the mechanical man had become the center of Hugo's life.

Hugo's father had owned a clock shop and worked part-time in an old museum taking care of the clocks there. One evening he had come home later than usual.

"Captain," he had said to Hugo, who was already in bed. "Sorry I'm so late, but I found something fascinating tonight at the museum . . . in the attic. Apparently, no one at the museum knows how it got there. Even the old guard doesn't remember, but then again he doesn't remember very much of anything. It's the most beautiful, complicated machine I've ever seen. It's a shame the museum didn't take care of it."

"What is it?" Hugo asked.

"An *automaton*."

"What's that?"

"It's a windup figure, like a music box or a toy, except it's infinitely more complicated. I've seen a few before, a singing bird in a cage and a mechanical acrobat on a trapeze. But this one is far more complex and interesting than those."

"What do you mean?" said Hugo eagerly.

"This one can *write*. At least I think it can. It's got a

pen in its hand, and it's sitting at a desk. I looked inside it and there are hundreds of little parts, including dozens of wheels that have edges cut with notches and grooves. I'm sure that if it were working, you could wind it up, put a piece of paper on the desk, and all those little parts would engage and cause the arm to move in such a way that it would write out some kind of note. Maybe it would write a poem or a riddle. But it's too broken and rusty to do much of anything now."

"Who made it?" Hugo asked.

"No one at the museum knows, but the other automata I've seen were all built by magicians for use in their performances."

"Magicians?" asked Hugo excitedly.

"Some magicians started off as clock makers. They used their knowledge of machines to build these automata to amaze their audiences. The sole purpose of the machines was to fill people with wonder, and they succeeded. No one in the audience could figure out how these mysterious figures danced or wrote or sang. It was as if the magicians had created artificial life, but the secret was always in the clockworks."

"*You're* a clock maker," said Hugo. "So you should be able to fix it."

"I don't know about that. It's pretty badly rusted and

pieces are missing. And I've got enough other things to fix."

Hugo was good with clocks, too. The talent ran in the family. Hugo's father had always brought home broken clocks for his son to play with, and by the time he was six, Hugo was able to fix just about anything. Later, when he visited his father at his clock shop, Hugo watched him carefully, and then when he grew restless he made little mechanical animals out of the extra bits and pieces lying around. Hugo's father displayed the creatures proudly on his workbench.

"Can I see the automaton?" Hugo asked. "Please."

A few nights later Hugo's father snuck him into the museum attic. In the dusty light Hugo saw broken model ships and heads of statues and old signs and piles of shattered doors. There were glass jars filled with strange liquids and stuffed birds and cats frozen midleap on a wooden stand.

At last his father lifted a stained white sheet, and there it was . . . the mechanical man. Hugo knew even then he would never forget the first time he saw it. The machine was so intricate, so complicated, that he almost got dizzy looking at it. Even in its sad state of disrepair, it was beautiful.

"You can fix it," Hugo whispered. "Don't you want to know what it can write? Then we'll wind it up and see what the message says."

"We'll see if I can get through my workload of broken clocks in the shop and at the museum, Hugo," said his father.

But even as he worked in his shop, Hugo's father must have kept thinking about the automaton.

Soon Hugo's father had filled several notebooks with drawings of the automaton. He opened the automaton up and carefully disassembled it. He drew detailed pictures of all its parts, then he cleaned them and patiently began to put it all back together. On Hugo's birthday, his father took him to the movies as he usually did, and he gave him one of the notebooks as a present.

Meanwhile, Hugo's father grew obsessed with getting the automaton to work. He brought Hugo back to the museum a few more times and explained how the mechanisms operated. They remained optimistic that it could be fixed, and they talked about what the automaton might write once it was working again. Hugo and his father began to think of the automaton as an injured animal that they were nursing back to health.

One night, the old guard in the museum forgot that Hugo's father was up in the attic, and he locked the door, trapping him inside.

Hugo had no way of knowing what happened next.

No one knows how the fire started, but it rushed through the whole building in minutes.

Hugo stayed up all night waiting for his father to come home. He had never been this late before. But when the door finally opened in the morning, it wasn't Father.

It was Uncle Claude.

"Pack your things quickly, Nephew," Uncle Claude had said, his breath smelling of alcohol as usual. Uncle Claude lifted his tiny steel spectacles with one hand and wiped his bloodshot eyes with the other. "Your father's dead, and as your only living relative, I'm taking you in."

Hugo, who hadn't slept all night, barely understood what his uncle was saying. He remembered hearing the blood beating hard in his ears, like the rhythm of a clock. In a trance, he put his clothes into a little suitcase, packed some of his tools and his deck of cards. He slipped his father's cardboard notebook into his pocket.

As they walked through the freezing streets of the city, his uncle explained about the fire and the locked door. Hugo wanted to fall over, to just lie down on the sidewalk and disappear. This was all his fault! He had wanted his father to fix the machine, and now, because of him, his father was dead.

"You'll be my apprentice," he vaguely heard his uncle saying as they walked. "You'll live in the station with me, and I'll show you how to take care of the clocks. 'Apprentice Timekeeper.' It's a good title for a boy. And besides, I'm getting too old to be climbing through the walls."

A million questions floated through the fog in Hugo's mind, but the only one that he finally said out loud was, "What about school . . . ?" Hugo's hand was still wrapped around the notebook in his pocket, and absent-mindedly he began to rub the cover with his forefinger.

His uncle laughed. "Ah, Nephew, you're lucky. You are finished with school. There won't be time for it once you're in the walls of the station. You should thank me." Uncle Claude slapped Hugo on the back and said, "You come from a long line of horologists. Your father would be proud. Now hurry up." Uncle Claude cleared his throat. He reached into his pocket, took out a greasy silver flask, and drank from it.

The word *horologist* had been painted on the door of Father's shop. Hugo knew it meant clock maker, and he had always thought he would be a clock maker like his father. But after the discovery of the automaton, Hugo began to have other ideas. He wanted to become a magician. Hugo began to think about running away, but at that moment, as if reading his mind, Uncle Claude grabbed the back of the boy's neck and didn't let go until they reached the train station.

And so Hugo began working all day in the dark on the clocks. He had often imagined that his own head was filled with cogs and gears like a machine, and he felt a connection with whatever machinery he touched. He loved learning how the clocks in the station worked, and there was a kind of satisfaction in knowing how to climb through the walls and secretly repair the clocks without anyone seeing him. But there was hardly ever any food to eat, and Uncle Claude yelled at Hugo, rapped his knuckles when he made mistakes, and forced him to sleep on the floor.

Uncle Claude taught Hugo how to steal, which Hugo hated more than anything, but sometimes it was the only way to get something to eat. Hugo silently cried himself to sleep most nights, and he dreamed of broken clocks and fires.

Soon, Uncle Claude began to disappear for hours at a time, leaving Hugo to take care of the clocks, twice each day, by himself. Sometimes his uncle didn't return until very late at night, and then one day, Uncle Claude didn't come back at all.

Hugo was afraid that his uncle would track him down if he left, but finally, on the third night that his uncle did not return, he decided to escape. He packed up his things and raced out of the station. He was hungry and tired and had no idea where he would go. He made his way through the narrow city streets, turning blindly, terrified he'd freeze to death before he found shelter. He looked down at his feet as he walked because the wind was bitter, and eventually Hugo found himself, quite by accident, in front of the ruins of the burned-down museum. All that was left of the building was a jagged brick wall with nothing behind the windows but black sky. The police had put up wooden barriers, but no one had begun to clean up the place. A huge pile of twisted metal, wooden planks, and crumbled bricks lay in front. And then something in the wreckage caught Hugo's eye.

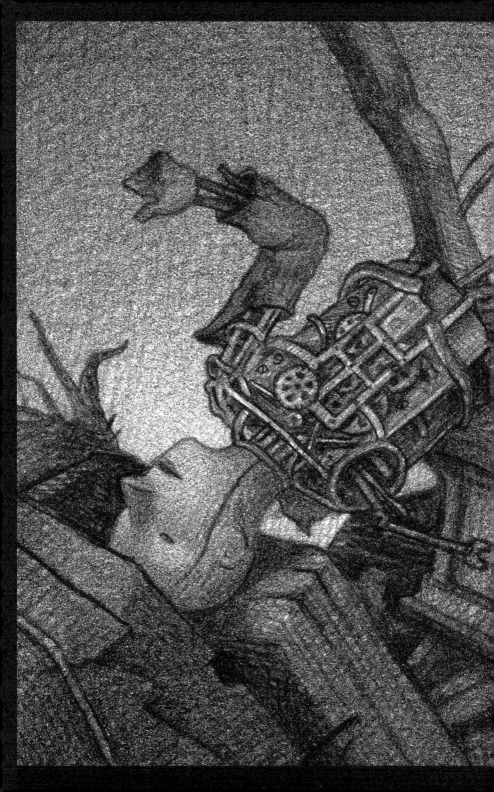

There it was, like an accusation, reminding Hugo that everything in his life had been destroyed. He sat down and stared at it.

A long time passed.

Dogs barked in the distance, and the rumblings of the street cleaners pierced the quiet of the night. Where was Hugo supposed to go? What was he supposed to do? He had no one. Even the automaton was dead.

He gathered up his few belongings and walked away. But he kept looking back at the ruined machine, and for some reason he couldn't leave it there. After all of his father's hard work, the automaton belonged to him. Hugo took a deep breath, went back, and cleared away the charred debris. The automaton was heavy and in several pieces, but he picked it up and, not having anywhere else to go, returned to the dreaded station.

It was a difficult trip back, with his belongings slung over his shoulder and the blackened, twisted remains of the automaton straining his arms and back. He didn't even know what he was going to do with this thing once he got it back to his room.

Since it was late at night, he managed to drop it inside one of the air vents without anyone seeing him. It took several trips through the walls to get it all back to his room. When he finished, his hands were scratched pretty badly, and his arms and back ached. Hugo laid out all the pieces on the floor and washed his hands in the basin by the bed, which he refilled from the spluttering sink in his tiny kitchen. He stared at the misshapen pieces of metal and was thankful that his uncle still hadn't returned.

"Fix it."

Hugo jumped. He could have sworn he heard a voice whispering in his ear. He looked for his uncle, but the room was empty. Hugo didn't know if it was his own thoughts, or if it was a ghost, but he had heard it clearly.

"Fix it."

Looking at the automaton, Hugo didn't think he'd be able to do it. It was in far worse shape than before. But he still had his father's notebook. Maybe he could use his father's drawings as a guide to rebuild the missing parts.

Increasingly, Hugo felt like he had to try. If he fixed it, at least he wouldn't be so completely alone.

Hugo knew it would be dangerous to stay at the train station. His uncle could come back, and in the meantime, he was sure that if the Station Inspector knew he was there alone, he'd be locked up in that little jail cell in the office and then sent off to the orphanage. Then the automaton would probably be thrown away or destroyed.

Hugo quickly realized he had to make it seem like his uncle was still around. He would keep the clocks running as precisely as possible, and he'd take his uncle's paychecks from the office when no one was looking (although he didn't know how to cash them). Most of all, Hugo would do his best to remain invisible.

Three months had passed since then. Hugo ran his fingers along the arm of the automaton and gazed at its face. He had studied the drawings in his father's notebook closely and had made great progress. He had repainted the face himself, and it had the strangest expression. It reminded him of Father, the way he always seemed to be thinking of three things at once. The newly polished wooden hand was now poised above the desk as it once was, waiting for Hugo to make it a new pen.

Hugo had continued thinking about the note that it would eventually write. And the more he worked on the automaton, the more he came to believe something that he knew was completely crazy. Hugo felt sure that the note was going to answer all his questions and tell him what to do now that he was alone. The note was going to save his life.

Whenever he imagined the note, he always saw it in his father's handwriting. Maybe Father, while he had been working on the automaton up in the attic of the museum, had changed the little mechanical parts just enough so that it would make a new note, one meant just for Hugo. It *was* possible, after all.

Now he just had to get the notebook back from the old man so he could finish his work and read the message from his father.

6

Ashes

THE NEXT DAY, AT THE CRACK OF DAWN, the old man was opening his toy booth when Hugo approached.

"I thought I might see you today," said the old man as he turned toward Hugo. He reached into his pocket and removed a tied-up handkerchief and held it out. Hugo's eyes widened hopefully. But as soon as he took the handkerchief, he understood what he had been given.

His breath caught in his throat, and tears began to form in his eyes as he undid the knot.

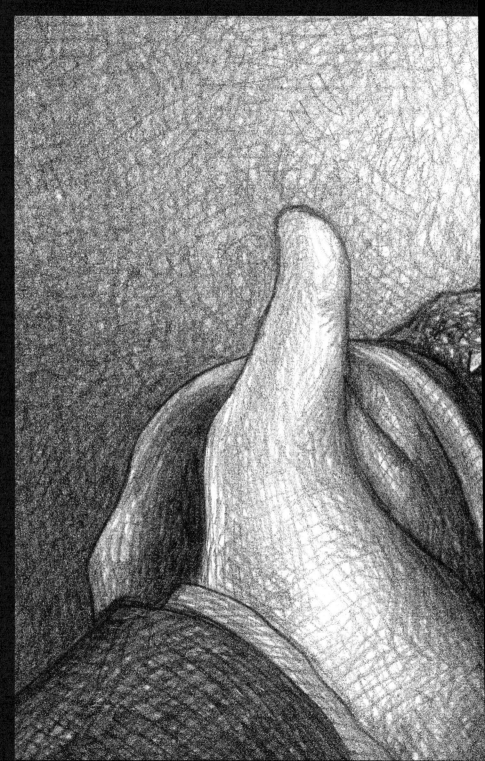

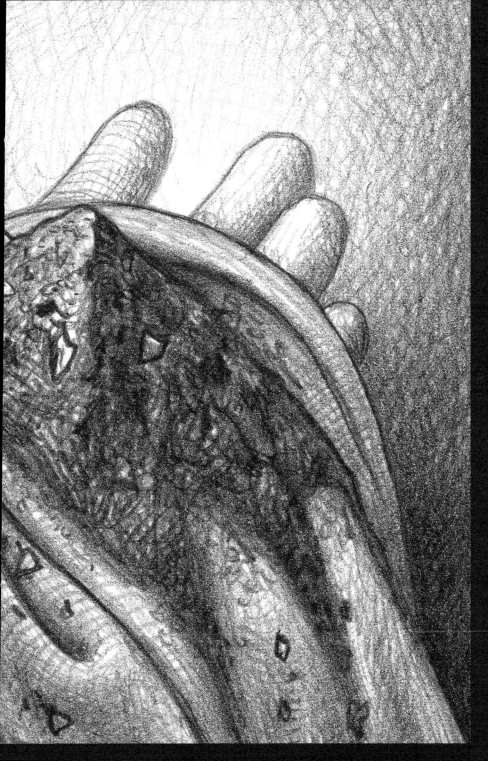

Hugo touched the ashes and then let them fall to the floor with the handkerchief. He staggered backward. All of his plans, all of his dreams, disappeared in that scattered pile of ash. Hugo charged at the old man, but the old man was quick and caught his arms.

"What is your attachment to this notebook?" he demanded as he shook Hugo. "Why won't you tell me?"

Hugo was sobbing. As he tried to release himself from the old man, he noticed something strange. The old man seemed to have tears in his eyes, too. Why in the world would *he* be crying?

"Go away," the old man whispered, letting go of Hugo. "Please just go away. It's over."

Hugo wiped his eyes with his dirty, ashen hands, leaving long black smudges across his face. He turned around and ran off as fast as he could.

Hugo was exhausted, but it was time to check the clocks again. For a moment he considered giving himself up. He'd never get the message from the automaton now, so he might as well turn himself in to the Station Inspector and be sent to the orphanage. At least there he wouldn't have to steal food and worry about the clocks breaking down. But the thought of losing the mechanical man was too much to bear. He had grown to love it. He felt responsible for it. Even if it didn't work, at least at the train station he had it nearby.

Hugo set to work on the clocks, but no matter how he tried to distract himself, he kept seeing the handkerchief filled with ashes. He was angry with the old man, and he would never forgive the girl for lying to him.

At the end of the day, Hugo put down his bucket of tools and sat next to the clock he had been checking. He placed the railroad watch in the bucket, pulled his knees up to his chin, and held his head in his hands.

The steady rhythm of the clock lulled Hugo to sleep, but he dreamed of fire and woke up with a start.

Frustrated and sad and finished with the clocks, he finally returned to his room and tried to sleep. But his mind wouldn't stop spinning, and so he reached for a scrap of paper and a pencil from one of the boxes near his bed. He sat down on the floor and drew pictures of clocks and gears, imaginary machines and magicians on stage. He drew the automaton over and over and over again. He kept drawing until his mind calmed down. Then he slipped the drawings underneath his bed, onto the big pile of other drawings he had done, and climbed fully dressed into bed.

Morning came, and the clocks were waiting, as always.

After Hugo had finished his rounds, he washed his face and hands in his basin. He was thirsty and longed for a hot cup of coffee. It was impossible to steal coffee since someone had to pour it, so he searched through his jars and came up with a few coins.

Hugo bought himself the coffee and sat for a moment at one of the empty café tables. He preferred to pay for what he could with the coins that he found each week, and he tried not to steal anything he thought people needed. He took clothes from the lost and found and scavenged the garbage for day-old bread. Sometimes he allowed himself to steal fresh bottles of milk or pastries when they were left outside the café early in the morning, as his uncle had shown him. The toys, of course, had been an obvious exception to his rule.

The coffee was hot, and as Hugo let it cool, he looked around the cavernous station at all the people rushing by with a thousand different places to go. When he saw them from above he always thought the travelers looked like cogs in an intricate, swirling machine. But up close, amid the bustle and the stampede, everything just seemed noisy and disconnected.

When Hugo picked up his coffee again, he noticed

that a folded-up piece of paper had appeared on the table. He looked around, but there was no one near enough to have left it. Slowly, he unfolded the paper.

It read: *Meet me at the bookseller's on the other side of the train station.*

That was all.

But then Hugo turned the paper over. There was one more sentence: *Your notebook wasn't burned.*

7

Secrets

HUGO HAD NEVER BEEN INSIDE the bookstore before, but of course he knew exactly where it was. He knew every inch of the train station. Opposite the café, not far from the main waiting room, there were two wooden tables covered in books flanking a door that read: R. LABISSE, BOOKSELLER, NEW AND USED.

A little bell jangled as Hugo stepped inside the store. He was rubbing the buttons on his jacket, and one came off in his hand. He slipped it into his pocket, where he continued to rub it. His heart was pounding.

The place smelled of old paper, dust, and cinnamon.

It reminded him of school, and a brief flash of his old life pleasantly filled his memory. His best friends, Antoine and Louis, both had black hair and liked to pretend they were brothers. Hugo hadn't thought about them in a while. The taller of the two boys, Antoine, used to call Hugo "Ticktock" because he always had clockworks in his pockets. Hugo wondered about them. Did they still pretend they were brothers? Did they miss him?

Hugo also remembered that sometimes at night, Father would read to him from amazing adventure stories by Jules Verne and a collection of Hans Christian Andersen's fairy tales, which were Hugo's favorites. He missed being read to.

A clerk sat at the desk, between two tall piles of encyclopedias. Hugo looked around. At first he didn't see anyone else in the shop, but then, like a mermaid rising from an ocean of paper, the girl emerged across the room. She closed the book she had been reading and motioned for Hugo to come over.

"Papa Georges still has your notebook."

"How do I know you're not lying? You lied before."

"I didn't lie. He's tricking you."

"Why are you telling me this? Why do you want to help me?"

The girl thought for a moment. "I want to see what's in your notebook."

"You can't. That's a secret," said Hugo.

"Good. I like secrets."

Hugo thought she was a very strange girl. She called to the clerk sitting at the back of the store, "Monsieur Labisse, I'm taking the book on photography. I'll bring it back soon."

"Yes, yes, fine, fine," he said distractedly as she left the bookshop without looking at Hugo.

Part of Hugo did not believe the girl. Maybe she was playing a trick on him. But since he had nothing to lose, he marched over to the toy booth and waited until the old man was finished with his customers. The cogs and gears in his head were spinning out of control.

"What are you doing here?" asked the old man.

Hugo took a deep breath. "I don't believe you burned my notebook."

"You don't?" The old man seemed surprised. He thought about it for a few moments and said, "Well, I don't really care. Maybe you're right, maybe those were not the ashes of your notebook, but you won't ever find out, will you?"

Hugo inched closer to the booth.

The old man calmly straightened the toys on the counter and said to the boy, "You should not have returned here, Hugo Cabret. Now go away."

Hugo did. But later, alone in his room, and while he scurried through the walls fixing the clocks, Hugo thought about the automaton. He convinced himself he had to keep trying. He returned to the toy booth the next day, and the day after that. At night, new drawings accumulated beneath his bed.

Finally, on the third day, the old man came at him with a broomstick. Hugo flinched, thinking that the old man was going to hit him. But instead he raised the handle toward Hugo and said, *"Be useful."*

Hugo took the broom and began to sweep the floor around the booth.

The old man watched carefully.

When Hugo finished sweeping, he handed the broom back to the old man. "Now give me my notebook."

The old man coughed and reached into his pocket. He pulled out some change. "Go buy me a croissant and a coffee, unless you're going to steal my coins, too."

Hugo happily grabbed the change and returned quickly, with two croissants and two coffees. They ate and drank in silence.

When they finished, the old man got up from the bench they were sitting on, went behind the counter, and found the remains of the little blue windup mouse that Hugo had stepped on when he was caught stealing from the booth. The old man laid the crushed pieces on the counter and said, "Fix it."

Hugo just stared at the old man.

"I said, fix it," he repeated.

"I need my tools," Hugo said.

The old man took out a small canister of tiny screw-drivers, pliers, files, and brass hammers. "Use these."

Hugo hesitated for a moment, but then set to work.

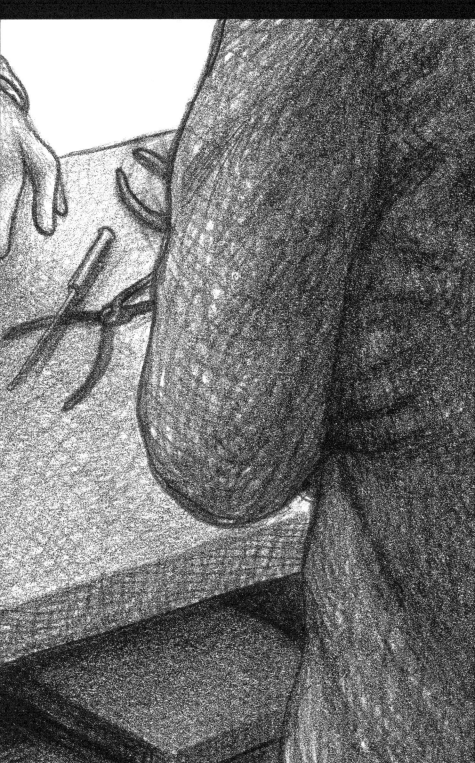

The mouse skittered noisily across the counter.

"So I was right about you," said the old man. "You've got some talent. Now will you tell me why you came to me? Will you tell me about the drawings in your notebook?"

"Give it to me first," said the boy.

The old man exhaled. "If I *didn't* burn your notebook, there's only one way I would even consider giving it back to you. Children like you are not worth the rags you wear, but most children like you would have disappeared completely after being caught. And most children like you aren't so good with mechanical things. Maybe you will prove that there is more to you than being a thief. Perhaps you can earn back your notebook. But remember, you are gambling with your time, because you might work for me for months and months only to find out that you were wrong about the notebook. There's a chance it's already gone. That's the risk you'll have to take.

"You'll come to the booth every day. I will decide how long you must work for each of the items you stole, and it will be up to me to decide when you have earned back your notebook, if it still exists. Do you understand?"

"I already have a job," Hugo said.

The old man laughed. "Thief is not a job title, boy."

"I have another job, but I'll come here when I can."

"You begin tomorrow," said the old man, and Hugo ran off down the empty hallway, careful not to click his shoe heels on the stone floor.

This wasn't the perfect plan, but for Hugo, at least it was a start.

8

Cards

AFTER MAKING HIS MORNING ROUNDS with the clocks, Hugo showed up at the toy booth the next day prepared to work. He could feel the cogs and wheels in his head spinning in different directions. One moment he felt hopeful that he'd get his notebook back, the next he felt angry and resentful. But he did his work. He swept the floor and organized the small boxes behind the counter. He untangled the wires of the flapping birds and repainted the chipped toys. He fixed the mechanical creatures that had stopped working.

Hugo found himself surrounded by more mechanical parts than he ever could have imagined. Everywhere he looked there were buckets of loose metal bits, tiny motors, gears, springs, nuts, bolts, and brightly colored tin. Hugo knew he shouldn't steal anything else, but looking at all these pieces was just too tempting. If he did get his notebook back he would need more parts.

He rubbed the buttons on his jacket and deftly pocketed the tiny mechanisms he wanted.

While Hugo worked, the old man played cards. Hugo's father had taught him how to play solitaire, and he used to entertain Hugo with a few card tricks. Hugo hadn't thought about that in a long time. As he watched the old man play, he saw things that captivated him. The old man didn't just shuffle the deck, he fanned it and flipped it and made the cards jump up into an arching bridge, shooting them in rapid succession from one hand to the other. He could cut the deck with one hand and make a second fan of cards appear behind the first. He even made a card float up by itself and then lower into the deck again. How could such a mean old man do such amazing things?

The next time Hugo came to work, he brought his deck of cards. After he had nearly finished his chores, he boldly went over to the old man and set it down.

"Show me how you do that with the cards."

"How I do what? Play solitaire?"

"How you make the cards fan out like that and float."

"Was I doing that?" the old man asked. "I wasn't paying attention. Now go work before I lose my patience."

Hugo didn't move.

The old man hesitated. He squinted at the boy with one eye, then picked up his cards and fanned them out in his hand again. He made them dance and rise and float.

Hugo stood, staring in delight, until the old man's voice shook him out of his trance.

"Enough. Go work."

But throughout the day Hugo stole glances at the old man, who continued to do amazing things with the cards. Sometimes Hugo caught his eye and got the distinct impression that the old man *wanted* him to see what he was doing, as though the old man was performing for him.

Eventually, the old man fell asleep again, and Hugo felt a tap on his shoulder. He turned and saw the girl with a bright red book under one arm. She put a finger to her lips.

"Meet me at the bookstore in ten minutes," she whispered. "Papa Georges doesn't want me here." Then she slipped behind benches and columns and disappeared down the hallway.

"I started looking for your notebook," the girl said when Hugo appeared.

"You better not look inside."

"If I find it I should at least be able to look at it."

"Then don't look for it." Hugo glared at her.

"I'm trying to help you. Why are you being so mean?"

Hugo blinked. He had never thought of himself as mean before. The old man was mean, not him. Hugo had no choice . . . he *had* to keep secrets, but he couldn't explain this to the girl.

She was standing there with her hands on her hips, looking at him with an expression he couldn't quite place. She looked very grown-up, like she was disappointed in him, and for a brief moment, quite unexpectedly, his heart sank. Hugo looked away from her and put his hands in his pockets.

"Just promise me you won't open it," he said.

"Fine." She sounded angry, but then she added, "If it falls open and I have to pick it up, I'm not going to close my eyes."

That's when the bell above the door jangled and a young man entered.

"Etienne!" the girl said.

"Hello, Isabelle," the young man said.

So her name was *Isabelle*, thought Hugo.

"I haven't seen you in a while. How are things at the toy booth?"

"Fine," said Isabelle. She motioned toward Hugo and said, "This is my friend . . . um . . ."

"Hugo."

Etienne smiled and took Hugo's hand.

"Etienne works at the movie theater near my home. He sneaks me in because Papa Georges won't allow me to see any movies."

"I always take pity on people who love the movies. I

can't help it. Do you like the movies, Hugo?"

"My father always took me to the movies for my birthday," he answered.

"What did you see?" asked Isabelle.

Hugo looked at both of them. He thought about the times he had gone to the movies with Father and how much they had loved being together in the darkness of the cinema.

Finally, Hugo answered Isabelle's question. "My last birthday we saw a movie with a man hanging from the arms of a giant clock."

"Oh, that's a good one! It's called *Safety Last,*" said Isabelle, "starring Harold Lloyd."

"I'm leaving town for a few days to visit my family," said Etienne. "But come by the movie theater next week when I'm back. I'll be working on Tuesday. I'll sneak you both in."

"I can't . . ." said Hugo.

"You must," said Etienne, smiling. "Promise you'll come."

"I can't do that."

"Come on, Hugo. Promise," Isabelle said.

The idea of going to the movies made Hugo remember something Father had once told him, about going to the movies when he was just a boy, when the movies were new. Hugo's father had stepped into a dark room and, on a white screen, he had seen a rocket fly right into the eye of the man in the moon. Father said he had never experienced anything like it. It had been like seeing his dreams in the middle of the day.

"All right. I promise," said Hugo.

Isabelle tucked her new book, *Greek Mythology,* under her arm and said, "Good. I'll see you then. I've got to go now. There's something I have to look for."

"Don't open the noteb—" said Hugo, but Isabelle was already headed toward the door.

"Good-bye, Etienne," she called. Then to Hugo she said, "I'll see you next week at the theater," and she disappeared into the crowded train station.

Etienne said, "Well, it was nice to meet you, Hugo," and he wandered off to find the book he had come in looking for. Hugo headed toward the door to leave, but the bookstore was warm and quiet, and the teetering piles of books fascinated him. He decided to look around for just a minute.

Hugo held the book that had caught his eye. There were golden cards embossed on the cover, as well as the title *Practical Manual of Card Magic and Illusions*. Inside, clear black-and-white diagrams revealed what seemed like an endless array of card tricks, many of which Hugo had seen the old man do. The second half of the book showed the secrets of how to make things disappear and how to throw your voice and pull rabbits from hats. More diagrams showed how to tear paper and have it reassemble itself, and how to pour water into a shoe and leave the shoe dry. Hugo continued flipping through the book, seeing if there was anything at all about automata, but the book was silent on the subject. Still, Hugo wanted it very much. He knew that Monsieur Labisse lent books to Isabelle, but Hugo didn't want to just borrow this one. He wanted to own it.

He slipped it under his arm and inched toward the door. He rubbed the remaining buttons on his jacket.

"Hey, Hugo," called Etienne, who was sitting on a stool reading. "What do you have there?"

Hugo grew agitated. He wanted to run, but Etienne approached him and took the book from under his arm. "Hmmm. Magic." Etienne smiled and handed back the book. "Do you know what's under my eye patch?"

Was Hugo really supposed to answer that question?

It seemed that Etienne was waiting for an answer.

Hesitantly, Hugo said, "Your eye?"

"No, I lost my eye when I was a kid playing with fireworks. A Portuguese Rocket flew into it."

Hugo thought about his father's favorite movie and wondered briefly if the man in the moon had to wear an eye patch after the rocket flew into his eye.

But all Hugo could think to say was, "Oh."

"So, do you want to know what's under my eye patch, then?"

"OK," said Hugo, thinking that what he really wanted to do was to get out of there.

Etienne reached beneath the eye patch and pulled out a coin, which he handed to Hugo.

"That's the only magic trick I know," said Etienne. "Go buy the book."

9

The Key

THAT NIGHT, AFTER ALL THE CLOCKS had been inspected and cleaned, Hugo opened the magic book. He read it from cover to cover, then reread his favorite parts, memorizing whole sections, practicing with whatever he could find around his room. But even as he fanned out his cards, or rolled a coin across the backs of his fingers, he found himself thinking about Isabelle. Hugo finally put the book down.

She said she would try to help him get his notebook back. Isabelle had called him her friend.

But how could he be her friend when he had so

many secrets? He didn't have any secrets to keep when he was friends with Antoine and Louis. He wished that Isabelle would just go away.

Before he got ready for bed Hugo took out the mechanical man and looked through all the little parts he'd stolen since he started working at the booth. Suddenly, it was as if a light went on in his head. Hugo saw how, with just a little work, one of the pieces would fit into the man's arm socket. He pulled out his tool kit and cut and filed the metal, bending it until it finally snapped neatly into place.

For the first time, Hugo had fixed something on the mechanical man without guidance from the notebook! His heart beat hard. What if he could fix the mechanical man *without* using the notebook? After all, who knew how long the old man was going to make him work? And what if the girl was still lying, and the notebook really was burned? He wasn't sure he could do it, but until the notebook was actually in his hands, he would try.

The week passed quickly. Hugo was more tired than ever. He hardly got any sleep because at the end of the day, after taking care of the clocks and working at the booth, he would stay up until dawn working on the automaton.

He made much progress, and he knew that he was getting very close to finishing.

When the time came to meet Isabelle and Etienne at the theater, he didn't want to break his promise, so he made excuses to the old man, left the station, and ran to the cinema. He snuck around back, where he found Isabelle waiting for him.

"Papa Georges must have hidden your notebook really well," she said, "but I think I might have an idea where it is."

Hugo wondered if he should remind her not to look inside it. He decided not to. "Why doesn't he want you to go to the movies?" Hugo asked.

"I don't know. Maybe he thinks it's a waste of time. He's never said why. I bet my parents would have let me go to the movies." Isabelle looked at Hugo, as if she was hoping he'd ask her a question about her parents, but he didn't, so she just kept talking.

"My parents died when I was a baby," said Isabelle, "and Papa Georges and Mama Jeanne were my godparents, so they took me in and raised me. They are very nice, except when it comes to the movies."

Hugo said nothing in response, so finally Isabelle said, "I wonder where Etienne is. He usually opens the door for me by now."

Hugo cautiously slipped around to the front of the theater and looked for Etienne. The manager of the theater, whose thin black hair was slicked across the top of his head, opened the door and said to Hugo, "What do you want?" The cigarette that dangled from his lips moved up and down as he spoke.

"I'm . . . um . . . looking for Etienne."

The man stared at him.

"He has an eye patch," said Hugo.

"I know who Etienne is," said the man as he smoothed his hair across his head and flicked his ashes toward Hugo. "I just fired him. We discovered that he was sneaking children into the theater. Isn't that a terrible thing to do?" He glared at Hugo.

Hugo backed away from the door, ran behind the theater, and told Isabelle what had happened.

"What an awful man. Follow me," Isabelle said. She walked to the rear door and took out a bobby pin from her pocket. Hugo watched as she fiddled with the pin inside the lock until it clicked and the door opened.

"How did you learn to do that?" asked Hugo.

"Books," answered Isabelle.

Isabelle poked her head inside to make sure no one was watching, then held the door open for Hugo. They entered the back of the lobby where photographs from upcoming films were tacked to a display case. Isabelle stopped for a moment and looked at one of the pictures, a black-and-white photograph of an actress with very dark eyes.

"Sometimes I think I like these photos as much as I like the movies," she said. "You can make up your own story when you look at a photo."

Hugo looked at the picture, but then Isabelle said, "Quick, the manager is coming." She and Hugo hurried from the lobby into the theater, sank down into the soft red-velvet seats in the back row, and waited for the movie to start.

The blank white screen reminded Hugo of a brand-new piece of paper, and he loved the wonderful whirring sound from the projector that filled the theater.

First came the newsreels, each one a few minutes long, about current events around the world. There was one about the Depression in America, one about a World's Fair that would be opening in Paris in a few months (Hugo thought that sounded exciting, although he knew he'd never be able to go), and one about politics in Germany. And then, finally, a cartoon began. It was called *The Clock Store.* In it, an old man was lighting streetlamps as night fell, and he passed a clock store. Inside, all the clocks were alive, and they were dancing to classical music. Hugo knew his father would have loved it. In the end, the music grew wilder as two alarm clocks had a fight. The curtains closed, everyone applauded, and the projectionist changed the reels. After a few moments, the curtains opened again and the main feature, *The Million,* by a director named René Clair, began. It was about an artist, a lost lottery ticket, a criminal, a borrowed coat, and an opera singer, and it had one of the most amazing chase sequences that Hugo could ever imagine. He thought every good story should end with a big, exciting chase.

Time passed quickly in the darkness, and as the lights came up, Hugo didn't want the afternoon to end.

He and Isabelle looked at each other, their eyes still shining from the flickering images. Everyone filed out of the theater until the children were alone in their seats in the back of the room. Hugo stared at the screen, as if he were still seeing the projected light, still hearing the sound.

Suddenly, Hugo and Isabelle were grabbed by their collars and hoisted to their feet.

"How did you two rats get in here?" the manager barked. Cigarette ashes fell on their heads. The children managed to take their coats and were dumped outside on the wet sidewalk in front of the theater. "And I better not see you here again." The manager closed the glass doors, wiped his hands, and glared at them until they ran away, brushing ash from their hair.

Once they were out of sight of the theater, they slowed to a walk. The air was cold and they shivered.

Isabelle told Hugo about other movies she loved: comedies and cartoons and cowboy movies starring someone named Tom Mix. There was an actress she'd seen named Louise Brooks who had a haircut that Isabelle had copied. There were adventure stories and mysteries and love stories and fantasies. She said names like Charlie Chaplin, Jean Renoir, and Buster Keaton. Hugo had seen a few Buster Keaton movies, and two

Charlie Chaplin movies, but for some reason he didn't share this with Isabelle. He just listened.

Soon they arrived back at the station. As they entered the waiting room, Hugo noticed someone standing very still, looking up at the main clock, taking notes on a clipboard.

It was the Station Inspector.

Hugo grabbed Isabelle and ducked behind a bench nearby. He rubbed the buttons on his coat.

"What are you doing?" Isabelle said, straightening herself up.

But Hugo was lost in thought. Had the Station Inspector begun investigating and found out that Hugo's uncle was gone? Hugo couldn't be taken away now, not when he was so close to finishing the mechanical man. He knew he shouldn't have gone to the movies. He never should have left the station.

Hugo's heart raced. He had to get into the walls to check the clocks, but Isabelle was still talking. He hadn't heard anything she had said for the last few minutes. When he thought it was safe, he got up and started walking in the opposite direction from the Station Inspector.

"Answer me, Hugo," she said as she caught onto his arm. "Don't just run away."

"I've got to go."

"That's what I mean . . . go where? I was asking you where you lived."

Hugo stopped short and stared at her.

"I don't know anything about you," she said. "You know where I live, you know about my parents. If we're going to be friends, then I think I should know about you. Why won't you tell me?"

Suddenly, Hugo started to run.

"Hugo!" she yelled. "Stop! Wait for me!"

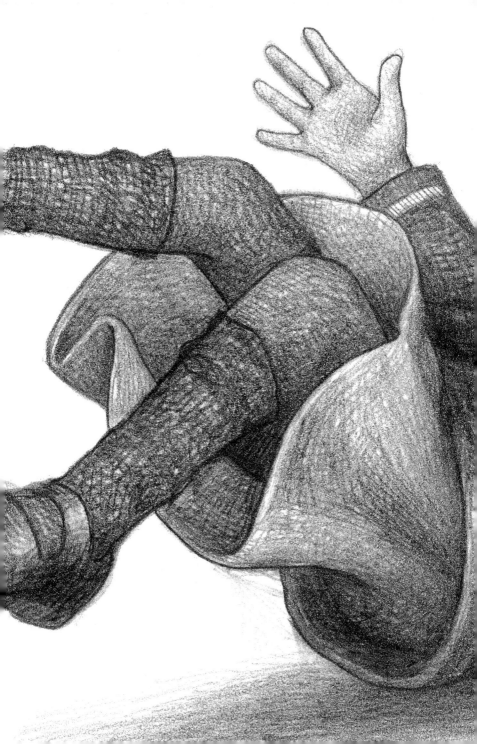

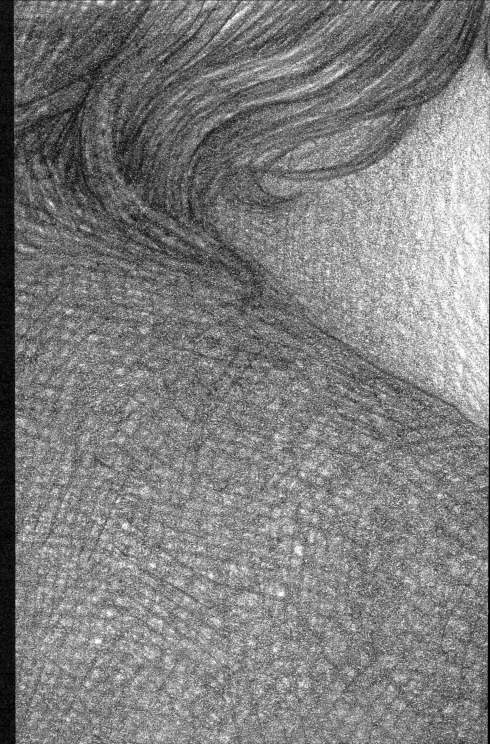

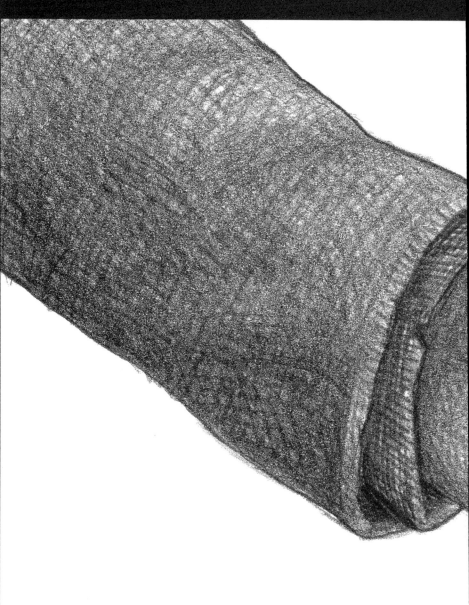

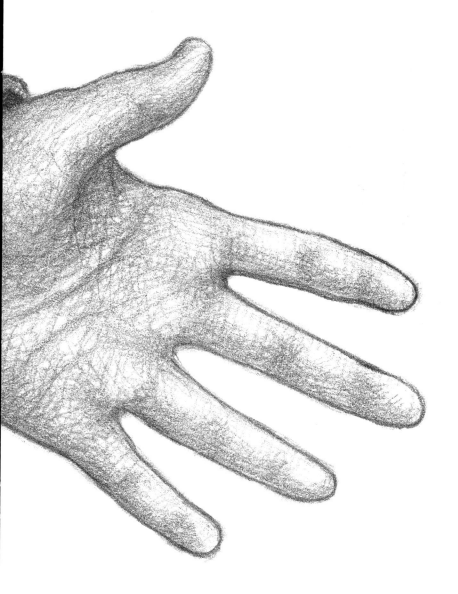

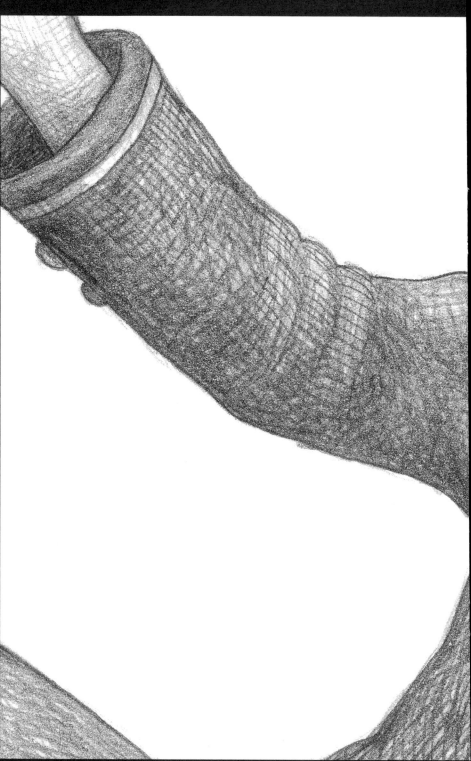

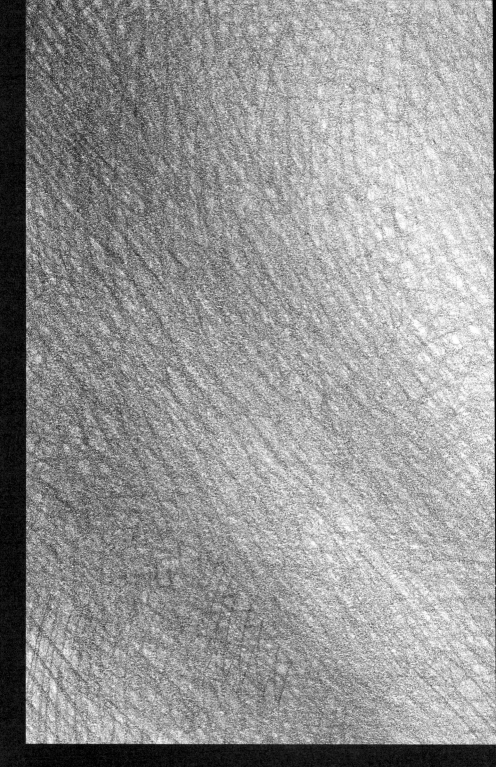

Hugo helped Isabelle to her feet, but he couldn't stop staring at the key. Isabelle noticed and tucked it back into her dress.

"Where did you get that?" Hugo whispered.

"Tell me where you live."

Neither of them said a word.

Without warning, Isabelle started running again, and this time Hugo chased *her*. Finally, she stopped at a café table and sat down, out of breath. Hugo sat down, too. One of the train station pigeons walked up to their table and pecked at some crumbs on the floor.

"Why are you so interested in my key?" Isabelle demanded.

"Tell me where you got it."

A steam engine whistled its deafening shriek, which completely drowned out all the other sounds of the station for a moment and made Hugo jump, as it always did. Hugo and Isabelle stared at each other until the owner of the café made them get up and leave. They parted without saying good-bye.

10

The Notebook

THE NEXT DAY HUGO WAS LATE getting to the toy booth. He ran his fingers through his dirty, disheveled hair and rubbed his eyes.

The old man looked up as he approached, put down his cards, and marched toward him. Hugo noticed that the old man's face was red.

He came at Hugo like a steam engine, seizing the boy by the arm. "Give it to me," the old man whispered fiercely.

"What?" asked Hugo in shock.

"How dare you break into my house!"

"What are you talking about?" asked Hugo.

"Where is it? Where is the notebook?" said the old man. "How did you get into my house? How stupid can you be? I was going to return the notebook to you! But what did you do after I took you in and gave you a chance? You repaid me with more theft, more lies. I watched you pocketing small mechanisms. Yet I didn't stop you. You kept the booth clean and were good at fixing the toys. You were helpful. My God, I even liked your company! But then you break into my house? I'm shocked you would even dare to show your face here again. You are nothing but a disappointment." The old man started coughing. He covered his mouth and pointed for the boy to leave.

At that moment, Hugo saw Isabelle over the old man's shoulder as she rose up from behind the counter. She stepped in front of the booth and raised one of her hands slightly.

She was holding the notebook.

Hugo said to the old man, "Let me say good-bye to Isabelle at least."

Isabelle hid the notebook behind her back.

The old man wiped his lips and said, "No! Now go away!"

But Hugo ran to Isabelle.

"I told you it wasn't burned!" she whispered. "What are those drawings?"

"I told you not to look. Now give it to me."

"No." She put the notebook into her pocket and kept her hand over it.

Hugo looked behind him. The old man was storming toward him. Without warning, Hugo wrapped his arms around Isabelle's neck and gave her a big hug. He could tell she was surprised.

"Let go of her," the old man said as he reached for Hugo's shoulder.

Hugo let go and dodged the old man's grip. Then he ran down the hallway without looking back.

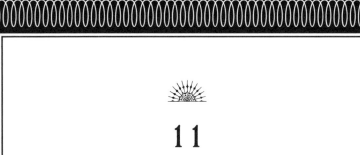

11

Stolen Goods

HUGO DARTED THROUGH THE CROWD, his vision blurry from tears, and made his way into the walls of the station. He hurried to his room, shut the door behind him, and lit some candles. Anxiously, he headed for the boxes that were piled near the wall and pulled out the mechanical man.

Hugo had indeed been busy in the last week. He had finally repaired all of the mechanical man's broken pieces and painstakingly loosened what was too rusty to move. He had sewed it a new outfit, and oiled and polished its mechanisms. The mechanical man was finally holding a brand-new handmade pen with a specially cut metal nib.

Hugo moved a candle closer to him.

In the middle of the mechanical man's back was a

heart-shaped hole, outlined in silver.

Since leaving the toy booth moments ago, Hugo's left hand had been clenched into a tight fist, which now he slowly opened like a flower.

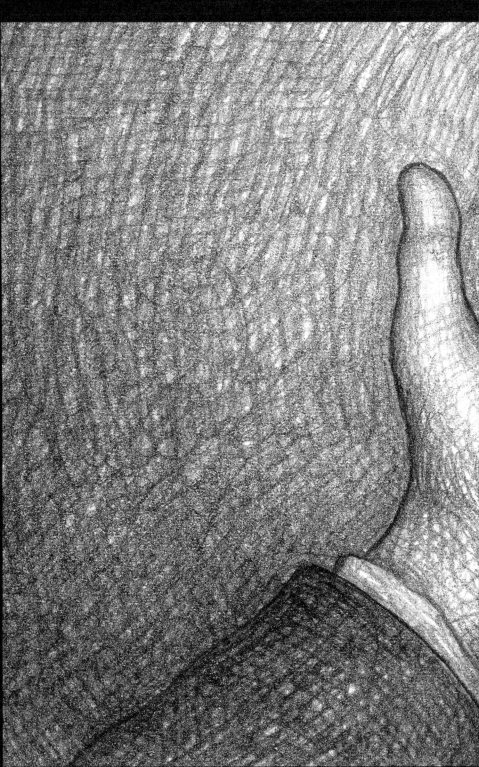

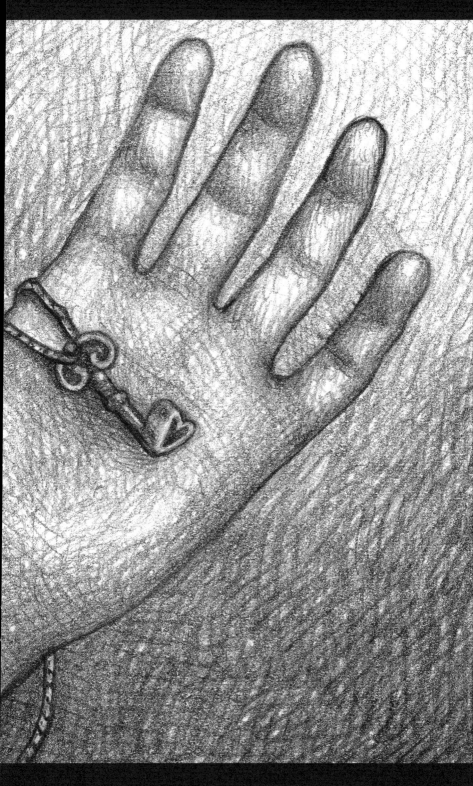

Hugo glanced over at the book that was sitting by his bed: *Practical Manual of Card Magic and Illusions.* He had been studying the book very closely and had learned how to do just about every magic trick it talked about. He found that he was quite good at them. With the proper instruction, his talent for machines translated perfectly to magic tricks. Hugo had come to understand the connection between horology and magic that his father had talked about. It wasn't just the understanding of machinery, it was the dexterity, the talent within his fingers themselves, as if they automatically knew what to do. Hugo's fingers were capable of the most surprising things. He had discovered that he could make cards float and he could turn marbles into mice and he could rip up a piece of paper and make it whole again. But most important, he found that with a hug good-bye, he could make Isabelle's necklace disappear without her feeling a thing.

12

The Message

HUGO'S HANDS WERE SHAKING.

He had managed to finish fixing the mechanical man. The only thing he had needed was the key. The original key had been lost in the fire, and all the other keys he found around the station and in the windup toys from the booth didn't fit. But when he saw the key around Isabelle's neck, he knew right away it would work. And now he had it.

He put the key in the heart-shaped hole in the middle of the mechanical man's back.

He had been right. It fit perfectly. Hugo's mind

raced. At last the time had come for him to get the message he had been waiting for.

But just as Hugo began to turn the key, he heard his door rattle. Before he could cover the mechanical man, the door burst open. Hugo didn't have time to scream as a dark figure lunged at him, knocked him to the ground, and landed on top of him. His head banged painfully against the floorboards.

"You stole my key!"

"What are you doing here? You aren't supposed to be here!" Hugo yelled.

"Why would you steal my key after I helped you? I got your notebook for you. I was going to give it to you! I just wanted you to promise to tell me about it. I should burn your notebook myself."

"Get out of here!" Hugo hissed into Isabelle's face. "You're ruining everything! Get off me!"

Using all his strength, he pushed her off and forced her toward the door, trying to get her out.

But Isabelle fought back. Soon she had pushed Hugo back down to the floor and was using her knees to keep him there. He yelped in pain, and she grabbed his wrists and pinned his arms to the floor. They were both breathing heavily.

"What is this place?" she said. "Who *are* you?" The

candlelight was reflected brightly in her fierce black eyes.

"It's a secret! I can't tell you anything."

"It's not a secret anymore! I'm here! Now tell me what this place is." She jabbed him with her knees, which hurt.

"This is where I *live*," Hugo spat back at her.

Isabelle didn't budge.

"Isn't that what you wanted to know? Well, now you know."

Quietly, Isabelle said, "Why should I believe you? You're a liar and a thief. Where is my key?"

In the candlelight, Isabelle hadn't yet seen the mechanical man sitting nearby. Hugo struggled beneath her, but it was no use.

Isabelle looked around for the first time. Finally, she saw it. She slipped off Hugo so she could get closer to the automaton, but she kept hold of one of Hugo's wrists.

"That's what was drawn in your notebook." She looked back to Hugo. "What's going on?"

The imaginary gears in Hugo's head began to turn.

"My father made it before he died," Hugo lied.

"Why would my key fit into your father's machine? That doesn't make any sense."

Hugo hadn't thought of that. "I don't know," he said. "I just knew your key would fit when I saw it."

"So you stole it," said Isabelle.

"I didn't know how else to get it," Hugo said.

"You could have asked."

Isabelle wiped her hair away from her face with her one free hand. "What happens when you wind it up?" she asked.

"I don't know. I've never had the key before."

"Well, don't just sit there," she said to him. "Turn it."

"No," said Hugo.

"What do you mean, no?"

"I . . . I want to be by myself when I turn it."

Isabelle looked at Hugo. She was clearly still angry. Letting go of his wrist, she pushed him back, grasped the end of the key, and turned it several times herself.

Hugo yelled out, but it was too late. "It needs ink!" he said. He quickly opened a bottle nearby and put a few drops in the tiny bottle in the automaton's hand.

The children watched as the clockwork gears and levers inside the man began to engage. They whirred and turned and spun. Hugo's heart raced. He didn't care anymore that Isabelle was sitting next to him. It didn't matter at all. The only thing that mattered now was the message.

A cascade of perfect movements, with hundreds of brilliantly calibrated actions, coursed through the mechanical man. The key tightened a spring connected to a series of gears that extended down into the base of the figure. There, the last gear turned a series of brass disks with precisely cut edges. Two little hammerlike contraptions came down and trailed along the edges of the notched disks, rising and falling as the disks steadily turned. The actions set in motion by the little hammers were then translated back up through a series of rods that led into the man's torso. There, the moving rods silently turned other mechanisms in the shoulder and the neck. The shoulder affected the elbow, and as the elbow engaged, it sent other movements in a chain reaction down into the wrist and, finally, the hand. Hugo and Isabelle watched, wide-eyed in wonder, as very cautiously the man's miniature hand began to move. . . .

Isabelle and Hugo held their breath. The mechanical man dipped the pen into the ink and began to write.

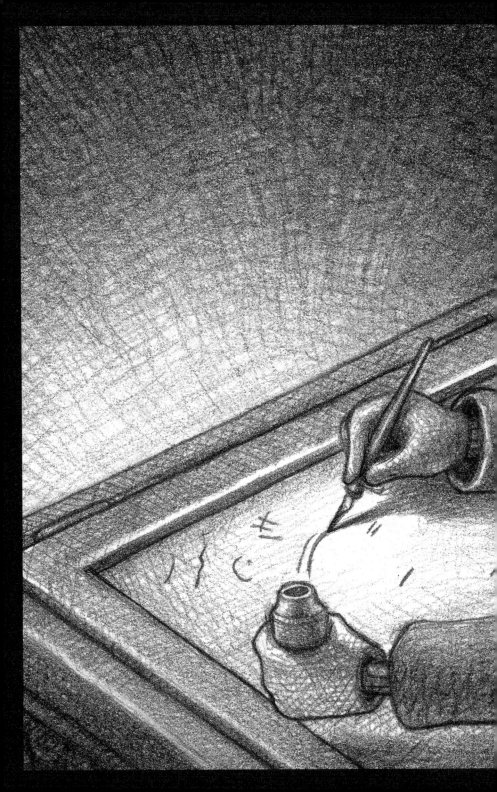

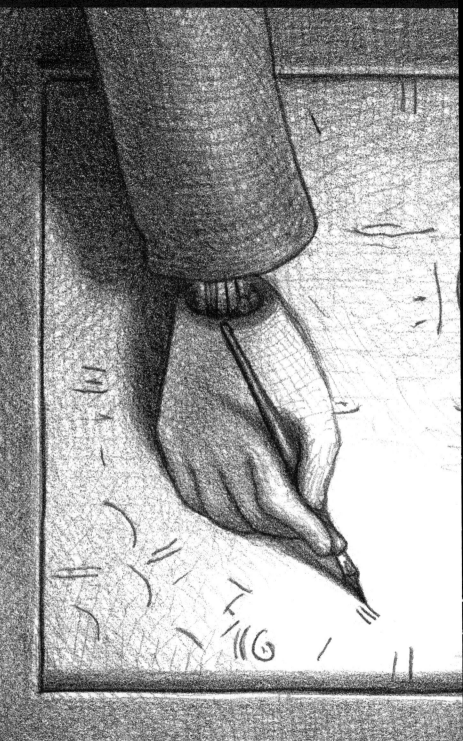

The children tried desperately to read it, but there were no letters, no words, no sentences, just random, disconnected markings. The mechanical man wasn't writing anything.

Hugo almost took the pen out of its hand because he was so upset. The automaton was not fixed. There must have been something Hugo had missed. He had failed.

"Give me my notebook," Hugo said fiercely to Isabelle.

Isabelle, startled by his intensity, reached into her pocket and handed it to him. He quickly grabbed the notebook out of her hands and did what he had wanted to do for a long time. Feverishly, he checked his work against his father's drawings.

He had done everything right. It should be working.

Suddenly, Hugo felt stupid for thinking he could fix it and especially for imagining there would be a letter from his father waiting for him.

All his work had been for nothing.

Hugo felt broken himself.

He stalked off to a dark corner of the room, put the

notebook down on a shelf, and buried his head in his hands.

But the mechanical man didn't stop what it was doing.

It kept dipping the pen into the ink and making more scratches on the paper. Isabelle stayed where she was, watching as these markings accumulated on the page, one after the other. The mechanical man's movements were so lifelike that its head even turned toward the inkwell as it dipped the pen for more ink.

And then something incredible happened.

Isabelle gasped. Hugo turned to look at her and then ran over.

He saw it immediately. The mechanical man hadn't just been scribbling. The lines were all coming together, like something in the distance moving into focus.

The mechanical man hadn't been writing . . . it was drawing!

It created an image that Hugo recognized immediately. Shivers ran down his spine.

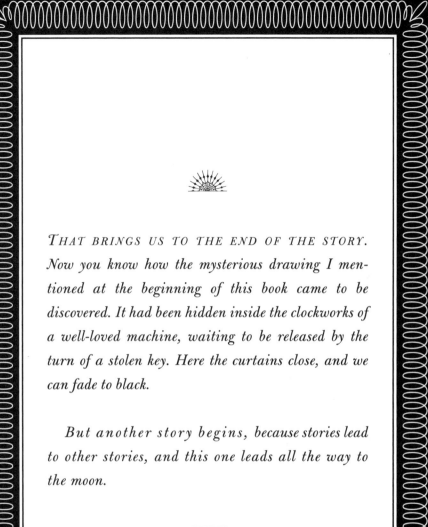

THAT BRINGS US TO THE END OF THE STORY. Now you know how the mysterious drawing I mentioned at the beginning of this book came to be discovered. It had been hidden inside the clockworks of a well-loved machine, waiting to be released by the turn of a stolen key. Here the curtains close, and we can fade to black.

But another story begins, because stories lead to other stories, and this one leads all the way to the moon.

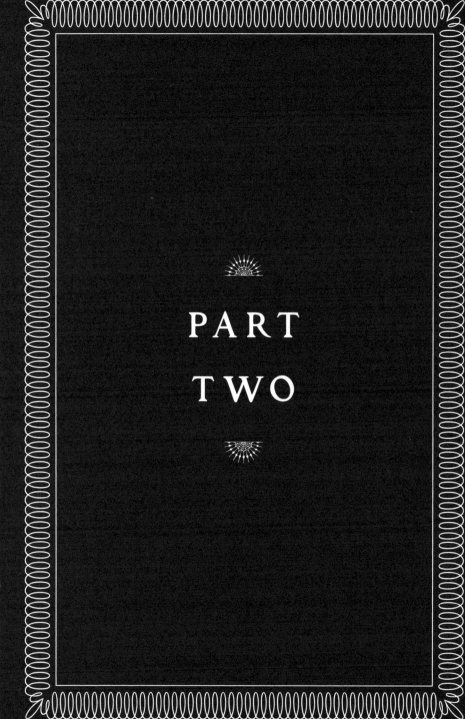

PART

TWO

1

The Signature

HUGO SAT TREMBLING beside the mechanical man. Of course he recognized the drawing. It was the scene his father had described from his favorite childhood movie. So Hugo had been right. The message was from his father. But what did it mean?

That's when the children realized that the mechanical man wasn't finished. It seemed to have stopped mid-line, as if it was pausing. Hugo watched as one more time the mechanical man dipped its pen into the ink. Then it moved its hand into position and . . . signed a name.

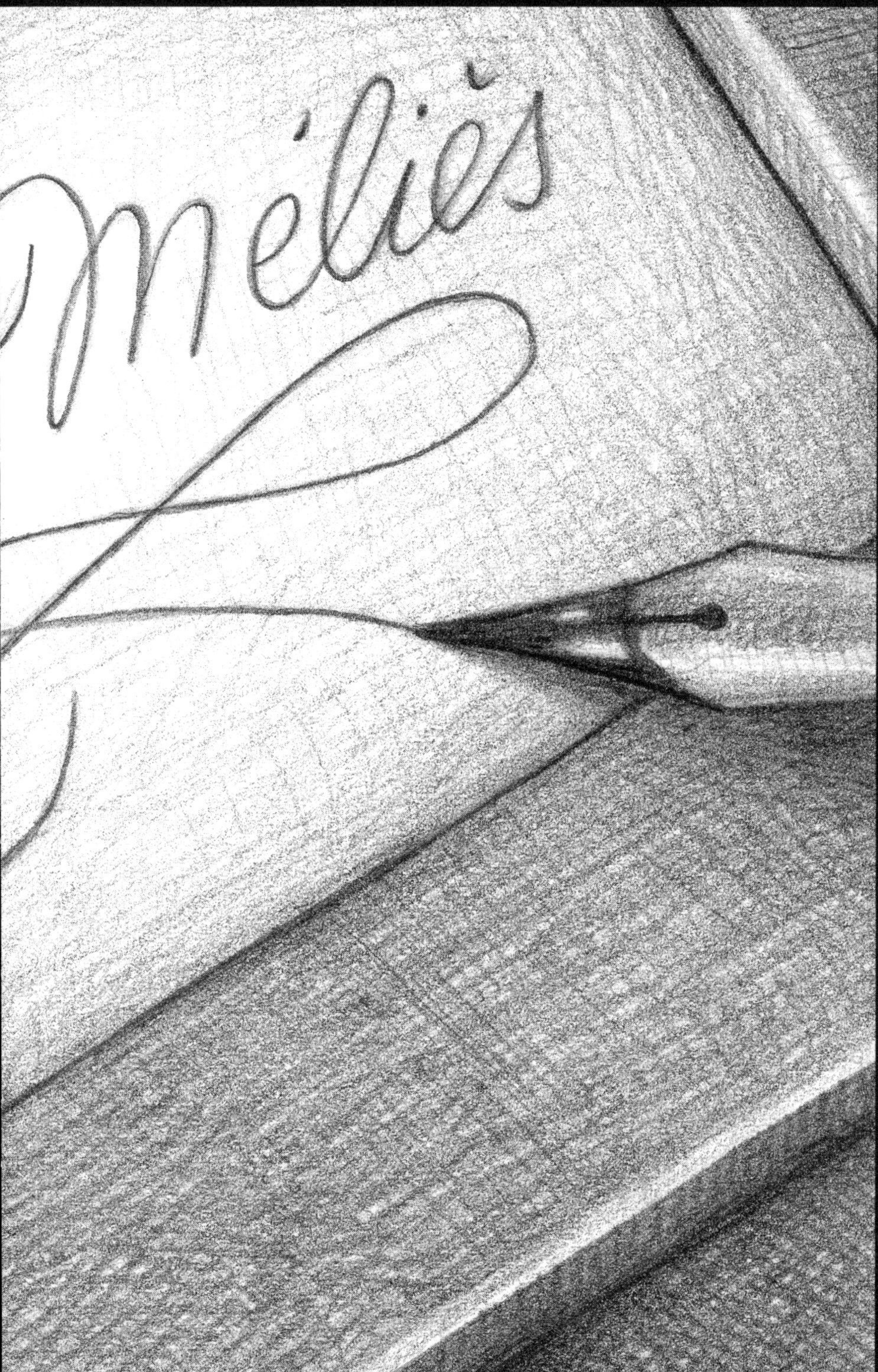
Méliès

"That's Papa Georges' name!" said Isabelle. She looked completely confused. "Why did your father's machine sign Papa Georges' name?"

She looked at Hugo in wonder, but then her expression changed and she glared at him. "You lied to me. This isn't your father's machine."

Hugo stared blankly ahead. This didn't make any sense at all.

"Are you listening to me, Hugo? This is not your father's!"

Hugo looked up at her and wiped his eyes. "Yes, it is," he said quietly.

"Then why did it sign Papa Georges' name? Why did my key fit into it?"

"I don't know," he answered.

"You are a liar!" yelled Isabelle. "You stole this machine from somewhere. You stole it from Papa Georges! The notebook probably isn't even yours. You must have stolen that, too!"

"I didn't steal it!"

"Liar," said Isabelle.

"It was my father's notebook. He drew it."

"I don't believe anything you say, Hugo."

Isabelle took her key from the mechanical man's back, put the necklace from which it dangled back around her neck, and grabbed the drawing from the little desk. "What are you doing?" Hugo said as he took hold of the paper in Isabelle's hand. "Give that to me."

"It has my godfather's name on it. It's mine."

The two of them struggled for the drawing and it ripped completely in half. After a moment of stunned silence, Isabelle took her half, got up, and started walking toward the door.

Hugo quickly pocketed his half of the drawing and chased after Isabelle, leaving the mechanical man in the middle of the room.

"Where are you going?" Hugo yelled.

"I'm going to ask Mama Jeanne what's going on. Stop following me!"

The children ran through the train station. It was late at night and the building was quiet. There was still a little time before the old man left the toy booth, so Isabelle hurried home as fast as she could. "Go away, Hugo Cabret," she called to him, but he was right on her heels.

Hugo knew he should have put the mechanical man back into its hiding place, and he should be checking the clocks, but there wasn't time now. As he followed Isabelle out the door, he prayed the Station Inspector had gone home for the night.

The children ran down the dark streets of the neighborhood and through the graveyard toward Isabelle's apartment. Hugo called after her, "Where did you get the key? Tell me that at least."

"No," said Isabelle.

"Did you find it? Was it a gift from someone?" Hugo caught up with her and grabbed her shoulder, spinning her around to face him. They locked eyes.

"Leave me alone!" Isabelle opened the door to her apartment building and pushed Hugo away. He reached for the edge of the door with one hand, trying to keep it open.

"Let go," she said. She pushed as hard as she could and slammed the door, crushing Hugo's fingers. Hugo heard an awful crunch and he screamed in pain. Isabelle screamed, too, and opened the door.

"What's going on down there?" shouted Isabelle's godmother from the top of the steps.

"You should have moved your hand!" whispered Isabelle.

"Isabelle? What's going on? Who's with you?"

Isabelle tried to push Hugo away, but seeing him cradling his hand under his arm, she shook her head and let him come upstairs. Tears were streaming down his face even though he didn't want to be crying. Isabelle slipped off her shoes before she went into the apartment, and she helped Hugo do the same. "No shoes in the apartment," she whispered. "And don't mention the mechanical man or the key," she added. "I'll ask her later, by myself!"

Isabelle's godmother clutched a silver brooch at her neck and said, "Who is this?"

"His name is Hugo, Mama Jeanne."

"The boy who's been working for Papa Georges? The one who stole from him?"

"He caught his fingers in the door downstairs."

"What is he doing here?" But before Isabelle could answer, the old woman led Hugo to the bedroom. "Come here. Let me see this in the light," she said. She moved the socks she had been darning and sat him down on a chair near the large wooden armoire underneath the lamp. She took his hand and tried to straighten his fingers. Again, Hugo screamed in pain. "You've hurt yourself pretty badly, young man." She disappeared for a few moments and came back with some chips of ice wrapped in a cloth napkin, which she handed to Hugo. "Here. Hold this on your fingers." Then she turned to Isabelle.

"I thought you were coming home tonight with Papa Georges."

Hugo was still angry that Isabelle hadn't told her

godfather she had stolen the notebook herself. And considering what she had done to his hand, he thought she should at least tell her godmother. But all Isabelle did was look at him. Hugo winced in pain as he balanced the ice on his bruised fingers, which were resting on his lap. With his good hand, he removed his half of the drawing from his pocket and said, "We have something we want to ask you."

"Not now, Hugo! I said not now!" yelled Isabelle. She tried to snatch the drawing away from her godmother, but it was too late. The old woman had already taken it.

"Where did you get this?" she asked in a stunned whisper.

"Give her the other half of the drawing, Isabelle," said Hugo.

Reluctantly, Isabelle reached into her pocket. She took out her half of the drawing.

Holding the two halves, Isabelle's godmother looked from the paper to the children.

"A mechanical man drew it," said Hugo.

"That's not possible. I don't understand," said the old woman, her eyes filling with tears.

"I have the mechanical man," said Hugo.

"You stole it, you mean," said Isabelle.

"You have the mechanical man? But . . . that can't be."

"I found it."

"What do you mean you found it?" Isabelle's godmother asked.

"I found it after the fire in the museum," said Hugo.
"I fixed it with pieces from your husband's toy booth.
And I wound it up using Isabelle's key."

"What key?"

Isabelle's face turned white.

"What key, Isabelle?"

Slowly, Isabelle reached into the neck of her dress
and pulled out the key on its chain.

"My key!" cried her godmother. "I thought I'd lost it!"

Tears formed in Isabelle's eyes. "I'm sorry, I . . ."

"You *stole* it?" said Hugo, shocked.

"It's the only thing I've ever taken, I swear, I just
thought it was pretty," Isabelle said to her godmother.
"Please don't be mad at me. I thought you wouldn't
miss it."

"Oh, heavens." The old woman brushed her hair
from her face. "I'm surrounded by thieves!"

She collected herself, wiped her eyes, and put down
the two halves of the drawing. Hugo quickly snatched
them up. A change came over the old woman as she
straightened her dress and said, "Take that drawing

away. We can't dredge up the past now. And whatever happens, don't let Papa Georges see it. And put the key back in your dress, Isabelle. You need to take good care of it." She wiped her eyes again.

Isabelle smiled slightly and tucked the key back into her dress.

"Please tell us what's going on," said Hugo.

"No. The only thing I'll say is that I need to protect my husband. And the best way for me to do that is just to forget about all this. Trust me. We must never speak of this again."

2

The Armoire

FROM THE BEDROOM WHERE THEY SAT, they heard the apartment door open. The old man coughed a few times as he entered. The old woman whispered to Hugo, "He can't know you're here. Just keep quiet, let him eat his dinner in peace, and then I'll divert him to the bathroom and you can sneak out. Now, I don't want to hear a noise out of either of you." Her eyes quickly glanced toward the armoire. It was a brief look, but Hugo and Isabelle had both seen her do it. She left the bedroom and closed the door behind her.

Hugo and Isabelle sat staring at each other for a few

moments, and then Hugo whispered, "She looked over at the armoire. There must be something in it."

"I already searched it when I was looking for the note-book," Isabelle said. "There's nothing."

"Search it again," said Hugo.

"Don't tell me what to do," said Isabelle, but after thinking about it she pulled another bobby pin from her pocket. Within moments she had unlocked the doors.

She looked again through the hanging coats and through the folded sheets and clothes on the lower shelves. She took the chair Hugo had been sitting on, stood on it, and checked the top shelves, but still found nothing. As Hugo looked up at her, he noticed something odd. There was a decorative panel at the top of the armoire, which had two thin parallel cracks in it. He pointed them out to Isabelle. She reached up and knocked on the wood. It sounded hollow. Still standing on the chair, she was able to get a grip on the wooden molding, and she pulled until the panel had come off in her hands.

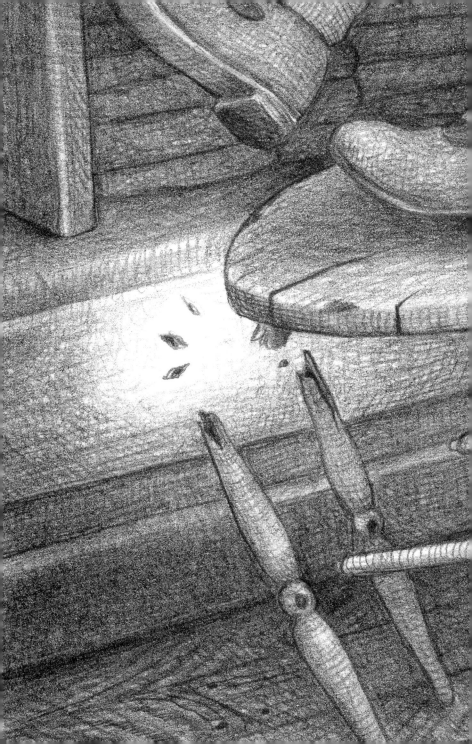

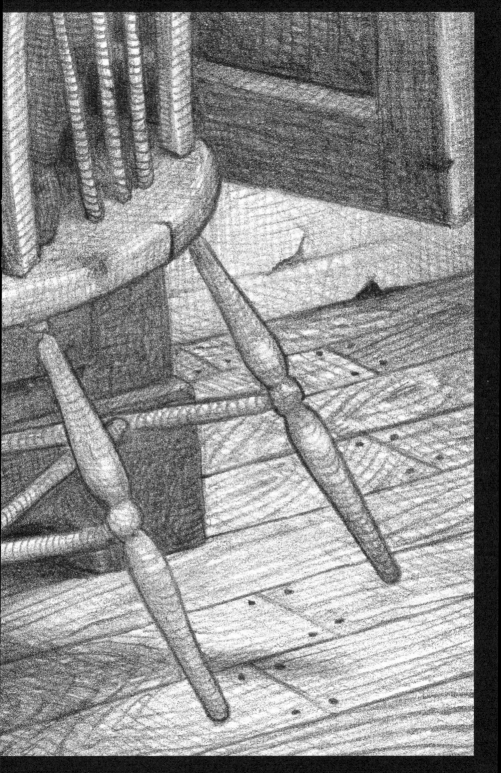

Isabelle shrieked and lost hold of the box. She landed on the floor, and the box landed on her foot and smashed to bits. She screamed again. The contents of the box flew everywhere. Hundreds of pieces of paper of every shape and size scattered across the floor. Hugo saw that they were all covered with drawings. Also inside the box was what appeared to be a very thin, old blanket, covered with images of stars and moons. It was frayed and dusty.

Within moments the bedroom door flew open. "Isabelle!" yelled her godmother as she ran to the girl.

The old man stood frozen in the doorway. He was staring at the drawings.

"Why would you do this, children, why?" wailed the old woman. "Hugo, gather up these drawings and lock them in the armoire." She handed him a key from her pocket. "Come now! Quick! And Isabelle, you come with me. Georges, go back out to the kitchen!"

Hugo pocketed the key and picked up the papers. He held them in his good hand as if they were diamonds and rubies. Some were on single sheets of paper, some hand-bound into little books. The edges of the drawings were yellowed and brittle, but they were all beautiful, and they were all by Georges Méliès.

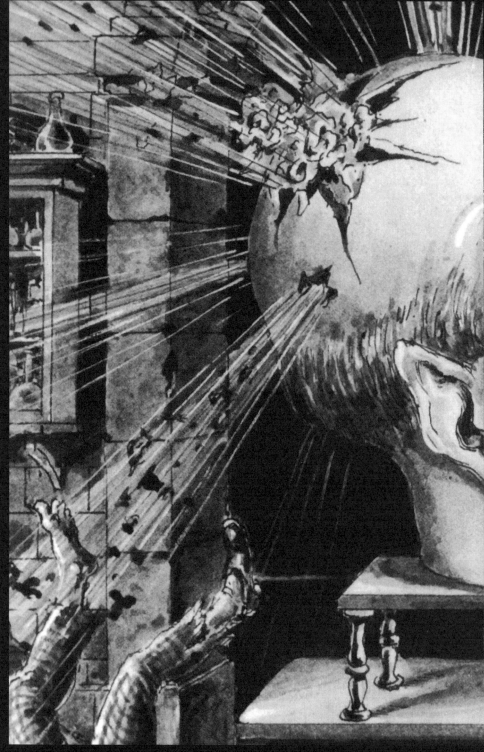

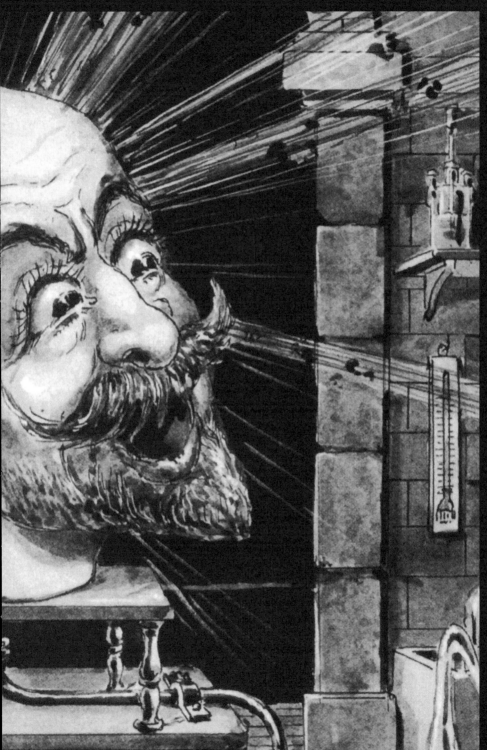

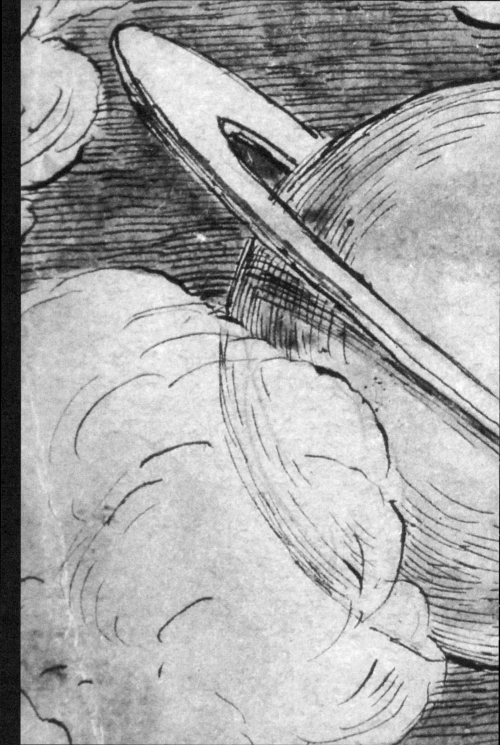

"No," the old man whispered to himself. "No. No. No. No! No!" His voice got louder with each word and he began to cough. "What is going on here? Where did these drawings come from?" He covered his eyes with his hands. "Who did those drawings? Who is playing this trick on me?"

"Leave the room, Georges!" cried the old woman, who was trying to help Isabelle stand.

The old man then ran toward the drawings and grabbed handfuls of them, tearing them apart. The children instinctively threw themselves onto his arms, separating him from the papers. Hugo's hand was in terrible pain, and Isabelle's foot felt like it was broken, but they tried desperately to keep the old man from destroying his drawings.

"Stop it, Georges! Stop!" yelled his wife. "This is your work!"

"HA!" he cried. "How could this be mine? I am not an artist! I am nothing! I'm a penniless merchant, a prisoner! A shell! A windup toy!"

While the old man was distracted by his wife, Hugo and Isabelle quickly gathered up all the drawings. They shoved them into the armoire and locked it.

The old man was now bent over the side of the bed, his face buried in his hands, weeping.

He was muttering the word *no* over and over again, and then he whispered, "An empty box, a dry ocean, a lost monster, nothing, nothing, nothing . . ." He continued to mutter and sob, and the children slowly backed away from him.

The old woman put her arm around her husband and helped him get into bed. She rested his head on the pillow and pulled the covers up to his chin. With tears running down her cheeks, she ran her hand softly along his rough white chin until his breathing had evened out and he was asleep.

"I'm sorry, Georges," she said, and kissed his cheek and turned out the light. She sat next to the bed, holding her husband's hand. "I'm so sorry."

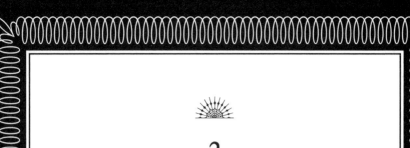

3

The Plan

HUGO HAD HELPED ISABELLE hobble out of the bedroom, and now they sat shaking at the kitchen table. He got some ice for her foot, and the two of them remained silent, trying to nurse their wounds.

Eventually, Isabelle's godmother came out of the bedroom.

"Are those really Papa Georges' drawings? Why didn't I ever know he was an artist?"

"Quiet, Isabelle. Just tell me how your foot feels."

"It hurts."

"And your hand, Hugo?"

He shrugged.

"My house has suddenly turned into a hospital ward." The old woman shook her head and tried to laugh, but she sat down at the table with them and began to cry.

"What's going on?" asked Isabelle. "Why were those drawings hidden in the armoire? Why did Papa Georges get so upset when he saw them?"

"Can't you see the damage that's already been done, Isabelle? Papa Georges is developing a fever. Who knows how long it's going to last. There's nothing more to say. You stole my key, you broke into my armoire. You're as bad as this thief here. I don't want you two to see each other again, do you hear me? You can stay here till the morning, Hugo. I'll call a doctor to look at you and Isabelle and Georges, and then I want you gone." She ripped up some strips of fabric and made makeshift bandages for Hugo's hand and Isabelle's foot. She wrapped them as tightly as she could.

"I'm sorry, Mama Jeanne! Please don't be mad. We just wanted to —"

"Hush. It's bedtime. Hugo, there is the couch. Come,

Isabelle, I'll help you to your room."

But Hugo didn't sleep on the couch. A plan formed in his mind, and as soon as Isabelle and her godmother had left the room and gone to sleep, he tiptoed over to the coat hooks by the door. The old man's coat was hanging there, and Hugo fished in his pockets. He heard a jangling sound and found what he was looking for. He took the ring of keys, left the house, and walked back to the train station in the dark.

Hugo headed straight for the shuttered toy booth. He made sure no one was around, and then he tried all the keys on the key ring until he found the one that opened the booth. He stepped inside and began going through the boxes, opening drawers, and flipping through papers the old man kept back there. But there were no clues. Hugo had been hoping that perhaps there might be some scrap of paper to help him figure out what it was the old woman was keeping secret, something in the booth he had never noticed before.

Hugo did find one curious item, though, wrapped in a piece of fabric at the very back of a drawer.

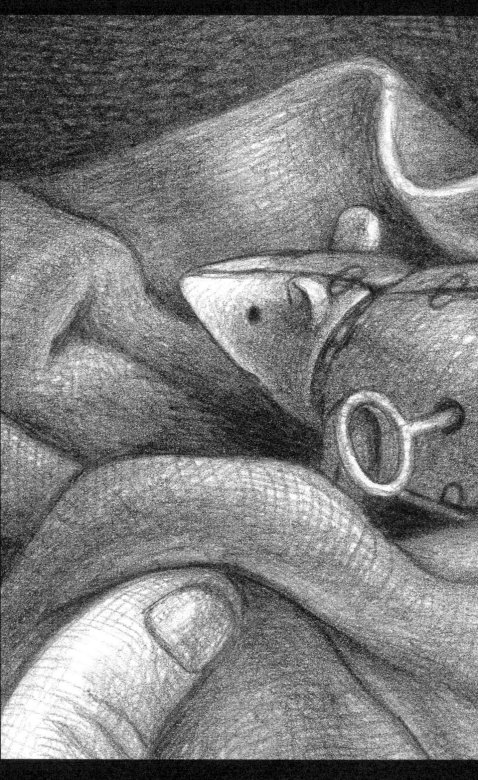

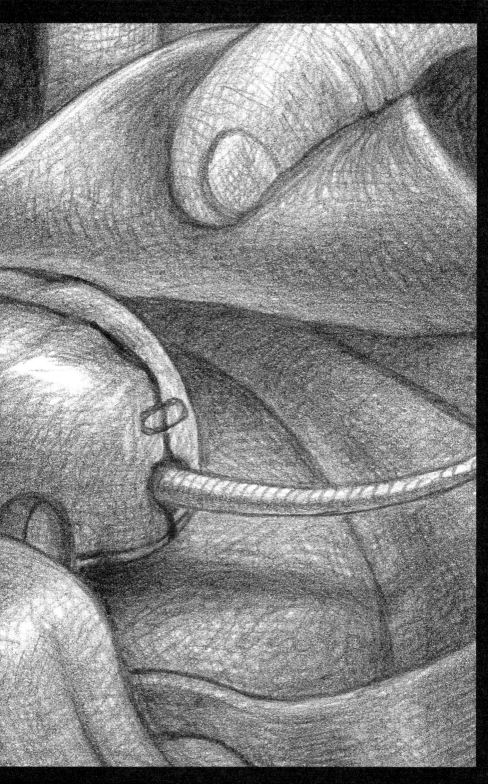

Hugo didn't know why the old man had kept the blue mouse. He had always assumed the toy had been sold a long time ago. Hugo liked that he had kept it, though. He found himself smiling as he turned the blue mouse over in his hands. Hugo thought about the little mechanical parts inside the mouse, as well as the other toys that he had stolen and used to fix the automaton. He had never really stopped to consider why the pieces from the old man's toys fit so well into the mechanical man.

Hugo wrapped up the mouse and returned it to the drawer. As he turned to leave, he saw one of Isabelle's books tucked into a corner of the booth. That gave him an idea.

Hugo returned to his room and was relieved to see the mechanical man still sitting in the center of the floor. He managed to drag it back to its hiding place, grimacing in pain the whole time. He wrapped it up once again in the old piece of fabric and covered the hiding place with boxes. When he finished, he glanced over at the shelf with his bucket of tools, and his heart pounded. He hadn't realized until this moment the trouble he was in. It was his right hand that had been injured, and there was no way he could take proper care of the clocks without it. Soon they would begin breaking down, and the Station Inspector would investigate and it would all be over.

Hugo lay down on his bed and rested his bandaged hand on his chest. Images flashed across his mind. . . .

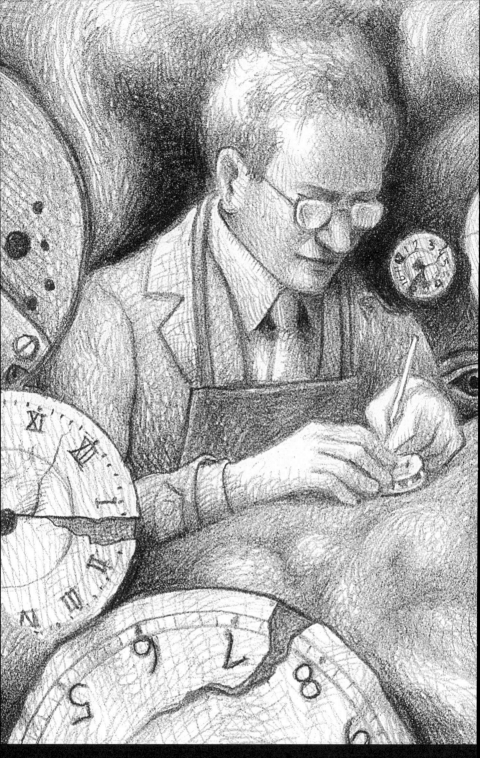

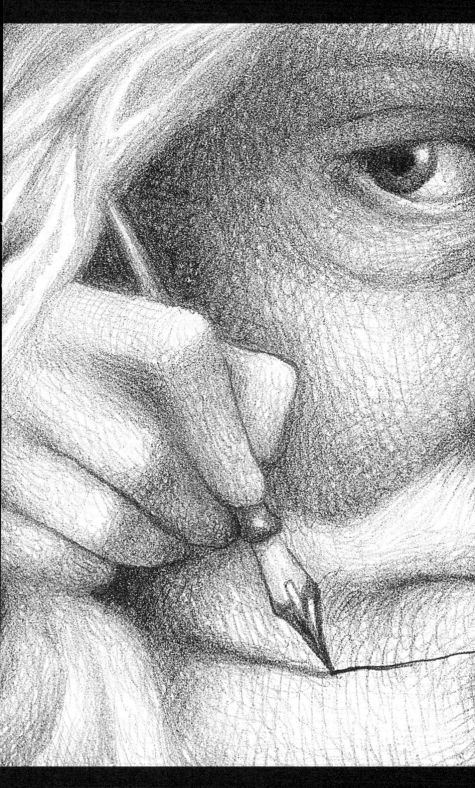

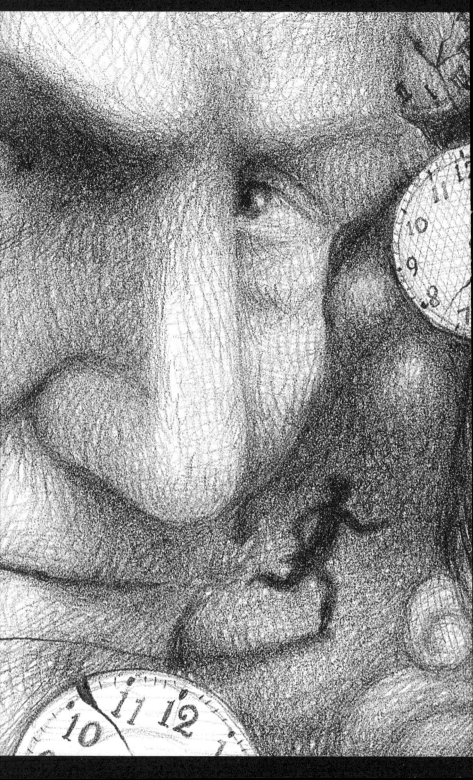

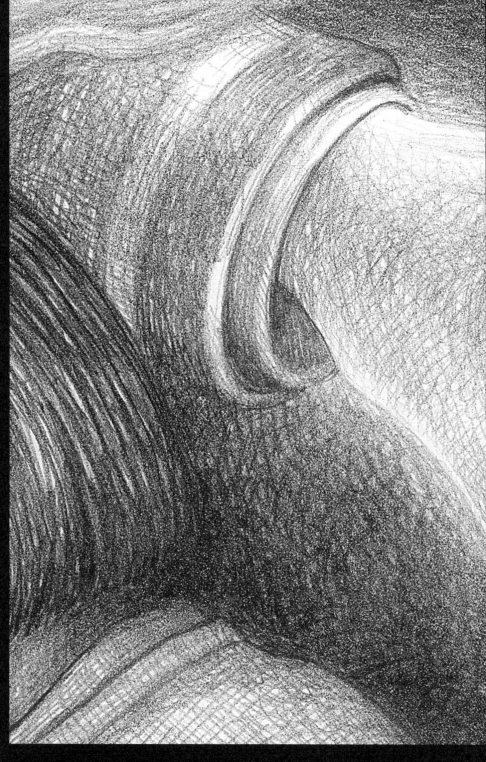

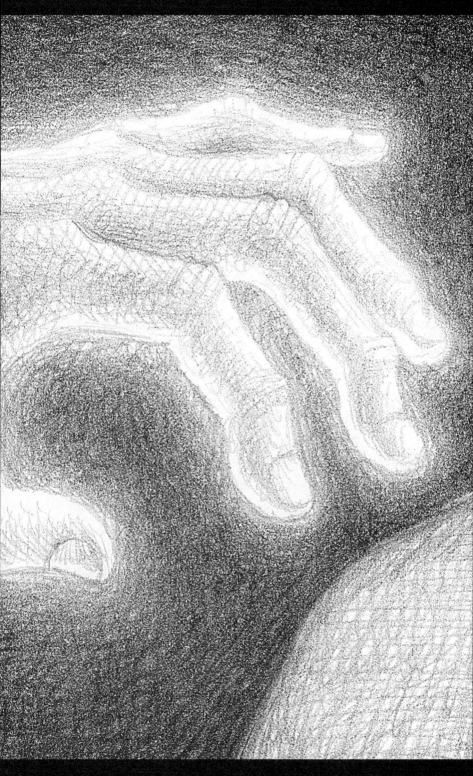

Hugo saw the white crooked fingers of the Station Inspector reaching for him. They turned into long ragged claws and grabbed him violently by the arm. Hugo woke up screaming. He hadn't even realized he had fallen asleep.

Morning finally came, and Hugo gathered up his tools and tried to do his morning rounds. Eyes closed, head tilted to the side, he listened to the clocks. But without the use of both hands, he could barely wind them, and so he oiled and observed as much as possible and anxiously compared the clocks with his railroad watch.

Time was running out.

As soon as he saw Monsieur Labisse open his shop, Hugo ran over. The bell above the door jangled as he entered.

Monsieur Labisse was still removing his coat when he turned and saw Hugo.

"You're Isabelle's friend, aren't you? What happened to your hand?"

Hugo moved his hand behind his back. "I need to ask you a question, sir. I need to find out information about something. Do you have books about the movies?"

"I might. . . ."

"What about the very *first* movies? My father saw a movie when he was little that he always remembered. It had a rocket going into the eye of the man in the moon." Hugo thought the movie would be a good place to begin his search for clues.

"That sounds intriguing," Monsieur Labisse said as he straightened his tie and stood up. "Come, young man." Hugo followed him to the shelf and waited while he looked through the books. He pulled out several volumes, glanced in the tables of contents, then closed the books and put them back. "No, no. Nothing about very early movies. I'm sorry."

Hugo thanked him and headed out the door.

Where could he turn next? The bookstore had been his big inspiration.

"You might have more luck at the Film Academy library," said Monsieur Labisse.

Hugo spun around. "Where's that?"

Monsieur Labisse gave Hugo directions, and Hugo thanked him and ran out of the shop.

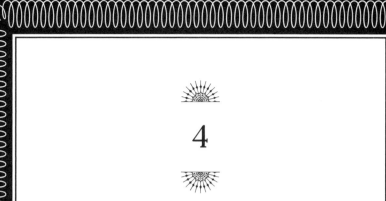

4

The Invention of Dreams

HUGO WAS STILL NERVOUS about leaving the station. But he took a deep breath and headed downstairs to the vast subway system that snaked beneath the city like hidden rivers.

Hugo entered the lobby, where a small woman sat at a big desk. He asked to use the library, and after looking him up and down in a disapproving manner, she said, "No."

"No?"

"You're too small and too dirty, and you must be accompanied by an adult," she said. "Good-bye."

Hugo just looked at her. He glanced at his hands and his clothes and realized that he hadn't thought about the way he looked in a long time.

Hugo knew the woman was being unfair, but he didn't know what to do about it. He was trying to figure out what to say, when he thought he heard his name being called.

"Hugo? Is that you?"

"Etienne!" Hugo ran to him. "What are you doing here?"

"I was just about to ask you the same thing."

The small woman at the desk looked at Etienne and said, "You know this filthy child?"

"Madame Maurier, this is my friend Hugo."

She pushed her black-rimmed glasses to the top of her nose and answered the phone, which had just rung.

"Sorry about your job at the movie theater," Hugo said.

"It worked out well, actually. When I was fired I had just started classes here, and they were able to give me some work in the offices. I'm studying to be a camera-man."

Hugo glanced at Etienne's eye patch and Etienne

smiled. "Having an eye patch actually makes it easier to look through a camera — I don't have to close one eye like everyone else."

Etienne tapped his eye patch and said, "Now tell me, what in the world brings you here?"

"I need to find something in the library. Can you help me?"

"Follow me," said Etienne. Hugo didn't look at Madame Maurier, but he was very happy to walk by her as they headed to the library.

The library was on the second floor. It was clean and orderly with rows of perfectly placed shelves, which seemed untouchable. In the center of the room was a large painting that caught Hugo's eye.

He didn't know what it meant, but he liked it.

Etienne helped Hugo navigate the card catalog so he could find the book he needed and then brought him to the correct shelf. Etienne stood on his toes, pulled the book off the shelf, and handed it to Hugo, who sat right where he was and opened it. Etienne sat down next to him. "You know, one of my teachers wrote that book. Will you tell me what you need it for now?" But Hugo couldn't talk. The book was called *The Invention of Dreams: The Story of the First Movies Ever Made.* It was written by René Tabard a year earlier, in 1930.

Hugo opened to the beginning of the book, and read:

In 1895, one of the very first films ever shown was called A Train Arrives in the Station, *which was nothing more than what the title suggests, a train coming into a station. But when the train came speeding toward the screen, the audience screamed and fainted because they thought they were in danger of being run over. No one had ever seen anything like it before.*

Hugo flipped through the pages of the book. There were images of men playing cards, people leaving a factory, each one a still from an early movie. Hugo continued turning pages, and then he saw what he had been hoping to find.

His father's favorite movie was called *A Trip to the Moon.*

The filmmaker Georges Méliès began his career as a magician and he owned a theater of magic in Paris. This connection with magic helped him immediately understand what the new medium of film was capable of. He was among the first to demonstrate that film didn't have to reflect real life. He quickly realized that film had the power to capture dreams. Méliès is widely credited with perfecting the substitution trick, which made it possible for things to appear and disappear on screen, as if by magic. This changed the face of movies forever.

*A Trip to the Moon, Méliès' most famous film,
followed a group of explorers as they went to the
moon, fought the moon men, and returned home
with a captive, to great acclaim. If one day far in
the future, mankind is truly able to fly to the moon,
we will have Georges Méliès and the movies to thank
for helping us understand that if our dreams are
big enough, anything is possible. Unfortunately,
Georges Méliès died sometime after the Great War,
and many, if not all, of his films are lost.*

"Died? He's not dead. . . ." Hugo said out loud.

"Who isn't dead?" said Etienne, who had been reading over Hugo's shoulder.

"Georges Méliès. He runs a toy booth in the train station."

Etienne laughed.

"I'm not kidding," Hugo said. "And he's Isabelle's godfather."

5

Papa Georges Made Movies

LATER THAT DAY HUGO RETURNED to his room with the book from the library under his arm. Etienne had arranged for him to borrow it. He read the book again and again, especially the part about Georges Méliès. He stared into the face of the man in the moon. Suddenly, he heard a loud knock on his door.

"Hugo? It's me, Isabelle."

Hugo jumped up and opened the door. Isabelle had

brought her own flashlight. She walked with crutches, and her foot was bandaged.

"What are you doing here?" he asked. "How did you even get here with crutches?"

"Everyone thinks I'm in bed. It took me a long time to climb out my window and make my way here."

They sat down on the bed, and Isabelle immediately started to cry.

"What is it?" Hugo said.

"I'm sorry I slammed your fingers in the door, and I'm sorry I didn't tell my godparents that I stole the notebook. I was mad at you for taking my key."

"Which you stole . . ." Hugo said.

Isabelle ignored him and kept talking. "And now Papa Georges is very sick. His fever is so high, and he's talking to himself. He just mumbles strange things like: 'a wingless bird, a burned-up building, a splinter, a fly, a grain of sand. . . .' I'm so worried about him. I've never seen him sick before. What if he dies?"

"He's not going to die," said Hugo.

"You don't know that! Papa Georges supports all of us! What would we do? Mama Jeanne called a doctor, who wrapped up my foot and gave us a prescription for Papa Georges. But with the toy booth closed, we have no money to get the medicine or for anything else."

"Everything's going to be all right," Hugo said. "But first I have to show you something." Hugo handed her the book from the Film Academy library, open to the page with the film still of the rocket in the moon's eye.

Isabelle stared at it in disbelief. "That's what the machine drew. . . ."

"Read it. . . ."

Isabelle read the pages about her godfather.

"Papa Georges made movies? I can't believe it . . . but he won't even let me *go* to the movies!"

"My father saw this movie when he was a boy," said Hugo, who pointed to the still from *A Trip to the Moon.* "He described this scene to me. I recognized it when the automaton drew the picture." Hugo told her about his trip to the Film Academy library and seeing Etienne again.

Isabelle put down the book. "Why did Papa Georges stop making movies? How did he end up at the train station?" She stretched out her leg. "Why didn't anyone ever tell me any of this?"

"Before I left the Film Academy library," said Hugo, "I told Etienne everything that was going on, and he brought me to meet his teacher, the one who wrote this book. I could tell that they didn't really believe me, so I, um . . ."

"What did you do?" asked Isabelle.

"I invited them to come to your apartment."

"You what?"

"Etienne and René Tabard are coming to your apartment next week. Monsieur Tabard wants to see your godfather for himself."

"Mama Jeanne will never allow the visit."

"Then don't tell her about it. Just wait till they show up."

"That's a very bad idea, Hugo."

"Well, I could cancel the visit, but I don't think we should. This is how we can find out everything. Don't mention this to your godmother yet. Don't tell her about the book or ask her any questions. Let's wait until Etienne and Monsieur Tabard come. Then she'll see that there are people who are happy her husband is alive, who remember him. And she'll answer our questions. I'm sure she will."

Isabelle shook her head. She looked very confused.

"You know, you never told me where you got the mechanical man."

Hugo had never told anyone the whole story. It had been his secret for so long that he wasn't sure he even had the words. But he looked at Isabelle, and it was as if he could feel all the cogs and wheels begin to engage in his mind, and the words suddenly came together. He related the whole story, from his father's discovery of the automaton up in the attic of the museum, to the fire, to the arrival and disappearance of his uncle. He told her about discovering the toys in her godfather's booth and how he used them to fix the automaton. He told her everything.

When Hugo finished, Isabelle was quiet for a few moments, then she said, "Thank you."

"For what?"

"For telling me."

"Come by the booth tomorrow after school. I have an idea."

"But the booth will be closed."

"No, it won't," said Hugo.

6

Purpose

THE NEXT MORNING HUGO OPENED the toy
booth and set it up exactly the way the old man always
did. His fingers were still hurting badly, but he smiled
as the customers straggled by and he collected the
money. Still, there were long stretches of quiet.

Hugo was frustrated at not being able to draw or
play with any of the mechanical parts. He tried to teach
himself to write with his left hand, but it didn't work. He
looked closely at the windup toys. He tried to imagine
what the old man was thinking as he built these toys.
He must have hated being stuck here all day long.

Maybe he was only happy for the time he devoted to building each new toy. Maybe they reminded him of building the automaton.

When Isabelle came by after school, she joined Hugo on a stool behind the counter.

Eventually, with no customers and nothing else to say, Isabelle tended to the loose ends of Hugo's bandages and took out a book. She began reading.

Hugo recognized the book. It was the collection of Greek myths she had borrowed from Monsieur Labisse.

"You've been reading that for a long time," said Hugo.

"Oh, I've read it twenty times. I bring it back to the bookshop, read other books, and then take it again. I like the stories."

"Read out loud."

Isabelle read the stories to Hugo, and he remembered hearing some of the myths when he was in school. She read about Mount Olympus and creatures like the chimera and the phoenix, and then read the story of Prometheus. Hugo learned that Prometheus had created humankind out of mud, and then stolen fire from the gods as a gift for the people he had made, so they could survive.

So Prometheus was a thief.

In his mind, Hugo suddenly saw the painting in the Film Academy library. One of the figure's hands was reaching up, holding a ball of fire, as if it were stealing the flames from above, and the other hand projected light, like it was a film. Hugo thought that maybe the painting was a version of Prometheus, except Prometheus was stealing fire from the gods to create the movies.

Isabelle continued reading the story. It turned out that Prometheus was punished for his theft by being chained forever to a rock where an eagle came to eat his liver, which grew back every day. Prometheus had stolen the fire because he wanted to help the people he had created, yet he was still punished. Hugo had become a thief to survive and to help the automaton. What would his punishment be? Was he now going to spend the rest of his life behind the counter of this toy booth like the old man? Was this all he had to look forward to? Hugo tried to push that idea out of his head. There had to be something else.

He found his attention being drawn to the clock across the hall. The big bronze hands moved slowly across the clock's face, like the sun across the sky. He wondered when it was going to stop running.

Hugo looked at his injured fingers and wished he would be able to use them again soon. He opened the drawer and pulled out the blue mechanical mouse, which he unwrapped carefully.

"What's that?" asked Isabelle.

"It's the toy I was stealing when your godfather caught me. I broke it, and he made me fix it. I don't know why he kept it."

"He must like you," Isabelle said. "In his dresser at home he has all the drawings I made him when I was little."

Hugo smiled, and then Isabelle wound up the mouse. They watched it skitter across the counter.

Hugo thought about his father's description of the automaton. "Did you ever notice that all machines are made for some *reason*?" he asked Isabelle. "They are built to make you laugh, like the mouse here, or to tell the time, like clocks, or to fill you with wonder, like the automaton. Maybe that's why a broken machine always makes me a little sad, because it isn't able to do what it was meant to do."

Isabelle picked up the mouse, wound it again, and set it down.

"Maybe it's the same with people," Hugo continued. "If you lose your purpose . . . it's like you're broken."

"Like Papa Georges?"

"Maybe . . . maybe we can fix him."

"How do we do that?"

"I don't know, but maybe René Tabard can help us when he visits next week. He'll know what to do. . . ."

Hugo and Isabelle were quiet for a moment, and then Isabelle said, "So is that your purpose? Fixing things?"

Hugo thought about it. "I don't know," he said. "Maybe."

"Then what's *my* purpose?" wondered Isabelle.

"I don't know," said Hugo.

The two of them stared at the clock, and then they put away all the toys, including the little mouse, and closed the booth. They collected the money they had made, and Isabelle put it in her pocket.

"Before you go home, come with me," Hugo said, and he helped Isabelle through the nearest air vent into the walls. Between Hugo's injured hand and Isabelle's sprained foot, it was extremely difficult for them to get up the staircases and the ladder, but they helped each other and at last they came to the glass clocks that overlooked the city. The clocks were supposed to be lit from the inside, but the wiring had long ago stopped working.

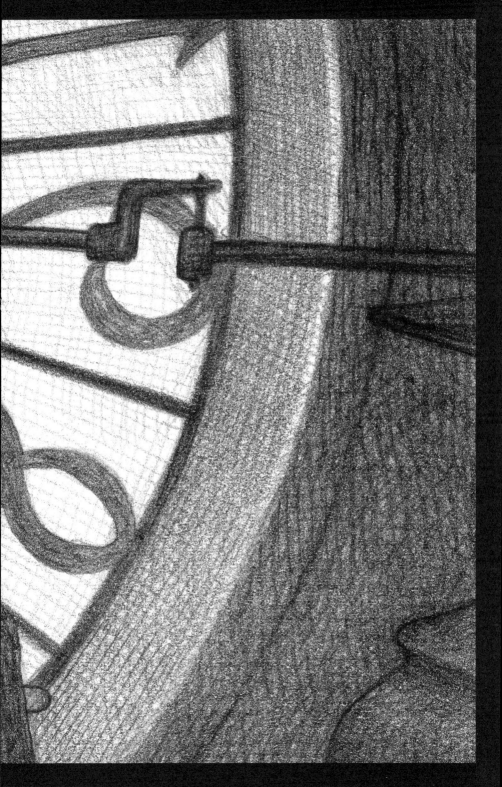

"It's so beautiful," said Isabelle. "It looks like the whole city is made out of stars."

"Sometimes I come up here at night, even when I'm not fixing the clocks, just to look at the city. I like to imagine that the world is one big machine. You know, machines never have any extra parts. They have the exact number and type of parts they need. So I figure if the entire world is a big machine, I have to be here for some reason. And that means you have to be here for some reason, too."

They watched the stars, and they saw the moon hanging high above them. The city sparkled below, and the only sound was the steady rhythmic pulse of the clock's machinery. Hugo remembered another movie he and his father had seen a few years earlier, where time stops in all of Paris, and everyone is frozen in their tracks. But the night watchman of the Eiffel Tower, and some passengers who land in an airplane, are mysteriously able to move around the silent city. What would that be like? Even if all the clocks in the station break down, thought Hugo, time won't stop. Not even if you really want it to.

Like now.

7

The Visit

Soon the children had raised enough money for the old man's medicine, which Isabelle bought at the local pharmacy. But it had been a difficult week. Hugo, as he walked through the station, watched the clocks begin to break down. They all had slightly different times. Most terrifying of all, the Station Inspector had written a note to Hugo's uncle and attached it to the latest paycheck, asking for a face-to-face meeting. Hugo didn't know what to do. He just kept praying that he could avoid the Station Inspector until his questions about the mechanical man had been answered.

At last it was the night before the visit from Etienne and René Tabard. Hugo could hardly fall asleep, and when he did, he dreamed about a terrible accident that occurred in the train station thirty-six years ago, which people still talked about. Hugo had heard stories about the accident from the time he was very young. A train had come into the station too fast. The brakes had failed, and the train slammed through the guardrail, jumped off the tracks, barreled across the floor of the station, rammed through two walls, and flew out the window, shattering the glass into a billion pieces.

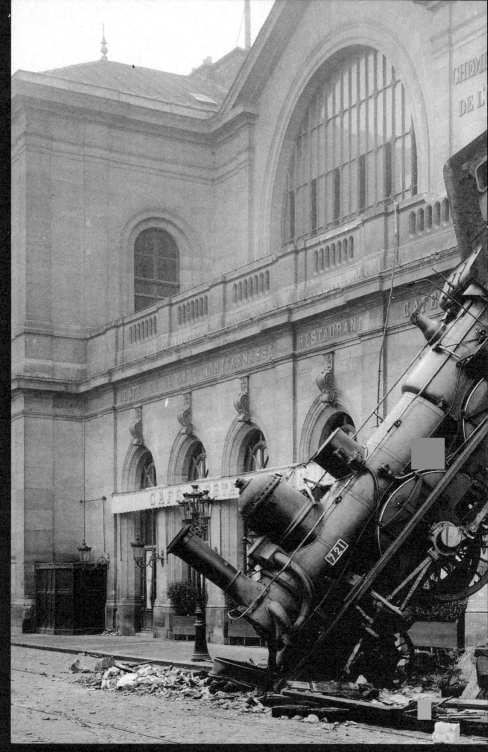

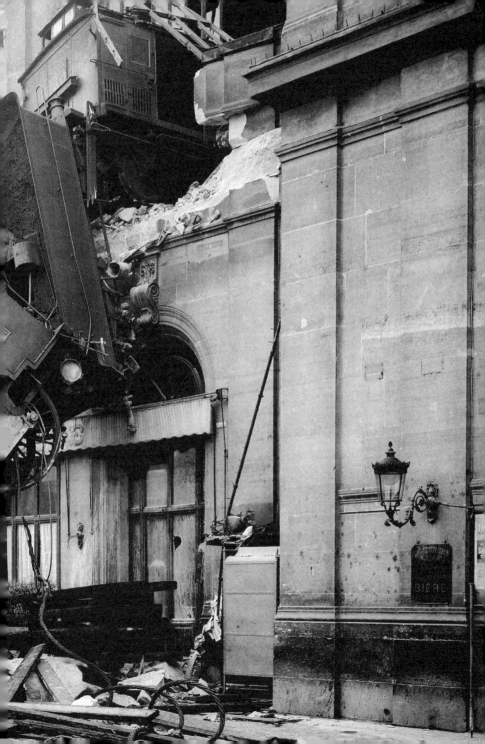

In his dream, Hugo was walking by himself outside the train station when he heard a loud crash and looked up. A train was falling on him from the sky.

Hugo woke in a sweat.

Hungry and afraid to go back to sleep, Hugo climbed out of bed and got dressed. He walked down into the train station and stole a bottle of milk. He was happy to find a tray of fresh croissants that had been left unattended near a delivery door. He took a couple of them and hurried back to his room, where he ate and waited until it was time for the meeting.

It was raining, and Hugo arrived just as Etienne and Monsieur Tabard approached with their two black umbrellas. Monsieur Tabard held some kind of large package under his arm. Isabelle called to them from the window and met them downstairs on her crutches. Both men closed their umbrellas and shook off the water before moving inside the doorway. Etienne hugged Isabelle, and she told them all to remove their shoes. "Papa Georges hates having shoes in the house."

Monsieur Tabard said, "Please tell me again your godfather's full name. . . ."

"Georges Méliès," said Isabelle.

"So it's true." He stared at Isabelle for a few moments,

then caught himself and said, "It's . . . very nice to meet you, young lady. I hope this is a good time for our visit."

"Yes," said Isabelle, "I think so. Papa Georges is feeling a little better."

"They are expecting us, are they not?" asked Monsieur Tabard.

"Um, please come upstairs."

Isabelle asked everyone to wait for a moment in the hallway, where Monsieur Tabard put down the large package he was carrying. Then, glancing nervously at Hugo, Isabelle entered the apartment. The visitors could hear voices, and finally, Isabelle returned and brought them inside.

"Please don't be mad, Mama Jeanne."

The old woman had been chopping vegetables, and she was holding a very large, shiny knife when she turned to see the three visitors enter her home. "Who are these people, Isabelle?" The knife glinted in the dull light of the apartment. Etienne and Monsieur Tabard took a step backward.

Hugo reached inside his wet jacket and took out the book that he had borrowed from the Film Academy. He handed it to Isabelle.

"We found out who Papa Georges was," she said to

her godmother. "Hugo found this book. It told us about his movies. Monsieur Tabard wrote the book, and Etienne is his student. Please, Mama Jeanne. They want to help. They love Papa Georges' films."

Monsieur Tabard straightened his bow tie and carefully stepped forward. "I deeply apologize. We thought you were expecting us. We will leave immediately and return upon your request."

The old woman, realizing she was brandishing a very sharp weapon, hastily put it down and wiped her hands on her apron. "Please keep your voices down, my husband is sleeping. I'm sorry. I . . . I wish that my goddaughter had told me about your visit, because we could have avoided this uncomfortable scene. I'm afraid I will not be inviting you back."

"Please, Mama Jeanne, don't make them leave."

"Madame Méliès, I don't want to impose on you,"

said Monsieur Tabard, "but if this is in fact to be the only time we meet, please let me tell you a brief story. I met your husband a long time ago, when I was a little boy. My oldest brother was a carpenter whom your husband employed on many of his earliest films. He often brought me with him to the studio where the movies were being made — I remember it like I was there just yesterday. I remember how the sun shone through all the glass. I thought it looked like a palace in a fairy story.

"One afternoon your husband appeared and shook my hand, and he said something to me that I've never forgotten." Monsieur Tabard paused for a moment, glanced toward the closed bedroom door, and then continued. "He bent down on one knee and whispered to me, 'If you've ever wondered where your dreams come from when you go to sleep at night, just look around. This is where they are made.'

"I grew up wanting to make dreams, too. Your husband gave me a great gift that day. I hope one day I can repay him."

Hugo remembered what his father had said about seeing his first movie as a child. He had said it was like seeing your dreams in the middle of the day.

The old woman lifted the bottom edge of her apron and wiped it across her brow. "I need to sit down," she said. Etienne brought a chair to her, and she sat with a sigh. "My husband was an important man, and I am pleased that you remember his films with such fondness, but he's become so fragile. It's not a good idea to dredge up the past for him."

"We brought some of that past with us," said Monsieur Tabard. "But if you don't think . . ."

"What did you bring?" asked Isabelle.

The old woman raised her eyebrows.

"When I was invited here to meet a man I thought had died, I must admit I was skeptical. But stirred by my memories of Georges Méliès, I sent Etienne down to the Film Academy archives, and in the very back, under a pile of old boxes, he found one of your godfather's movies. It's a little dusty, but I think it's in pretty good shape. We brought a projector with us, in case he wanted to see it. We figured it might have been a long time since he's seen one of his films."

Hugo and Isabelle grabbed each other. "Show us," said Hugo.

"No, no. I don't want to wake up Georges," said the old woman.

"Oh, please, let's watch it now. Please!" said Isabelle.

The old woman looked toward the closed door of the bedroom and touched the brooch at her neck. Her eyes shimmered momentarily with curiosity. At least that's what Hugo thought he saw. She covered her eyes with her hands as though the light was too bright, then she shook her head and said, "Be quick with it."

Monsieur Tabard and Etienne got the package from the hallway and unpacked the projector. They set it up on the table and took out the film reel. Etienne threaded the film through the projector and plugged the machine into an electrical outlet. Hugo closed the curtains. They aimed the projector toward one of the walls and turned it on. It clattered to life, and then the film began moving through it as light burst onto the wall. Images appeared, including Georges Méliès himself, as a young man, dressed in a fake white beard and a black cape covered with stars and moons. Hugo recognized the designs. When it had fallen out of the broken box in the armoire, he had thought the black fabric was a blanket, but now

Hugo realized it was a costume from the movie *A Trip to the Moon*. Hugo thought the movie was the most wonderful thing he had ever seen. He imagined his father, once upon a time, as a little boy, sitting in the dark, watching this very same movie, staring into the face of the man in the moon.

When the film was over, the end of it whipped noisily around and around the take-up reel until Etienne turned off the machine and the rectangle of light disappeared. Everything was silent.

But then the floorboards creaked, and they all turned. Georges Méliès was standing in the bedroom doorway with tears in his eyes.

"I would recognize the sound of a movie projector anywhere," he said.

His wife was crying, too. She walked over and put her arm around her husband.

"Who are these people?" he said.

Isabelle introduced him to Etienne and Monsieur Tabard.

"Monsieur Tabard teaches at the French Film Academy," she said, "and Etienne is one of his students. They are fans of yours." The two of them shook his hand.

"What are they doing here?"

Isabelle explained about the automaton and how Hugo had saved it from the fire. "He fixed it, and . . . I'm sorry . . . I did a bad thing. I stole a key from Mama Jeanne. But Hugo saw the key around my neck and realized it would fit in the automaton. We wound it up and the machine drew a picture, and then we found out everything. . . ."

Her godfather smiled. "Not everything, I'm sure."

Hugo reached into his pocket and took out the automaton's drawing, which he had taped back together, and handed it to the old man, who took it in his shaking hands.

Everyone was silent for a long time.

"Give me the projector," the old man finally said.

"What?" asked his wife.

He walked over to the machine and unplugged it. He lifted it up and carried it into his room. Then he shut the door and locked it.

8

Opening the Door

THE OLD WOMAN KNOCKED ON THE DOOR. "Georges? What are you doing?"

Everyone waited anxiously, but the old man didn't answer. There was no noise at all coming from inside.

"Georges," the old woman said as calmly as she could, "please unlock the door." She knocked again, but still he didn't answer.

Suddenly, there came a crash that was so loud they all felt it in their bones.

Everyone jumped and ran to the bedroom door. It sounded as if the door of the armoire was being ripped off its hinges or the dresser was being overturned, or worse, the old man had fallen and smashed his head. There was another moment of silence, but then they heard footsteps crashing back and forth across the room, and words they couldn't understand. The old woman threw herself against the door. "Georges! Georges! I'm sorry! Please let us in!"

Everyone continued to hear terrible sounds: things

being dragged across the room, banging and hammering, and low guttural noises, interspersed by periods of quiet. The children were terrified, and Isabelle's godmother was sobbing. Etienne and Monsieur Tabard tried forcing the door open, but it wouldn't budge. The noises grew louder and more terrifying.

All of them tried to push against the door, but it was no use. Finally, Hugo remembered. "Isabelle, pick the lock!"

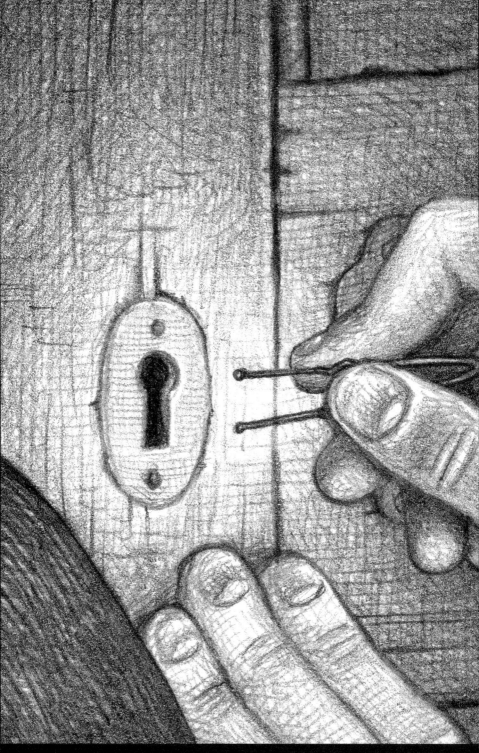

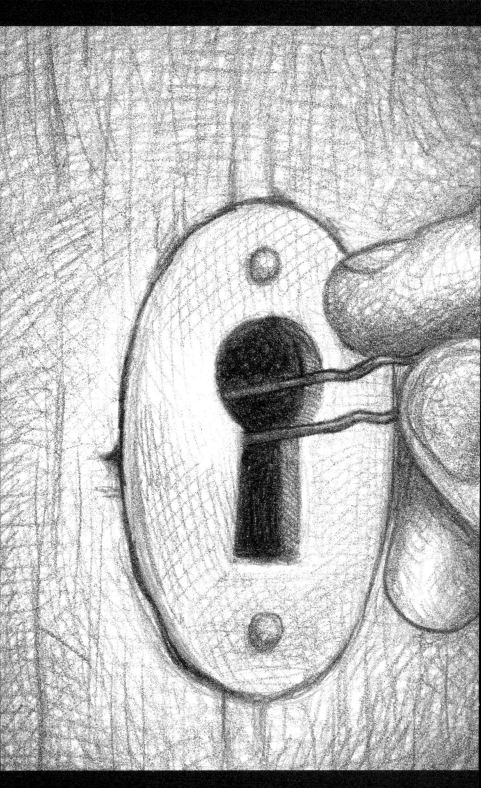

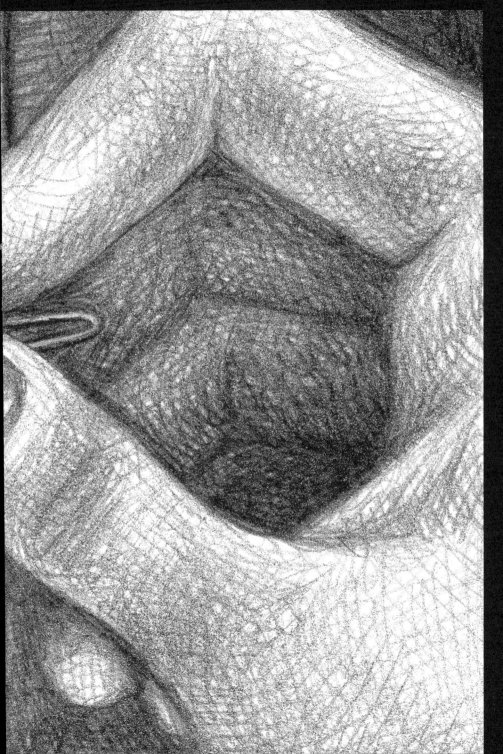

They pushed the door open, and the five of them stood there, expecting to see a huge mess, ripped-up drawings, chaos. But that's not what they saw at all.

The bed had been pushed to the side. Georges Méliès was sitting at a desk that he had dragged to the center of the room, a pen poised in his hand as though he were a giant version of the automaton. Hugo could see the automaton's drawing on the desk. The old man had broken off the armoire doors to get to his old drawings, and now they completely covered the floor, radiating from the foot of the desk, creeping up over the bed and across the walls, where they had been tacked all the way up to the ceiling. The curtains were drawn shut and the projector was sitting on one of the bedside tables that had been pulled over so it faced him from the doorway. From the projector, the film flickered across the entire wall. Images of the moon and the rocket and the explorers shimmered across the old man's face and onto the sea of his beautiful drawings, tacked to the wall behind him.

"My parents were shoemakers, did you know that?" he asked as he looked toward Hugo and Isabelle.

"They wanted me to work in their factory, but I hated shoes. The only thing I liked about it was the machinery. I taught myself how to fix the machines, and I dreamed about getting away and becoming a magician. So when I was finally old enough I sold my share of the factory and bought a magic theater. My wife was my assistant. We were very happy. I had a special workroom in the back where I built my automaton, and my audiences loved him.

"Then the Lumière brothers invented the movies. I immediately fell in love with their invention, and I asked them to sell me a camera. The Lumière brothers refused my request, so I was forced to build my own, which I did using leftover parts from my automaton. I soon found out that I wasn't the only magician to turn to cinema. Many of us recognized that a new kind of magic had been invented, and we wanted to be a part of it. My beautiful wife became my muse, my star. I made hundreds of movies, and we thought it would never end. How could it? But the war came, and afterward there was too much competition, and everything was lost. I hated telling all my employees that I couldn't support them anymore. And just when I thought it couldn't get any worse, two of my dearest friends, a young cameraman and his wife, were killed in a terrible car accident. But their baby daughter survived."

"Me?" said Isabelle.

"You."

"My father made movies with you?"

"Your father was the cameraman on my last several movies. Your mother was a teacher at a local school, and I loved them very much. After they died, you came to live with us. . . . You were the only bright spot in a very dark world. I made my wife promise she would never talk about my movies again. I shut the door on my past. . . . I burned my old sets and costumes. I was forced to sell my movies to a company that melted them down and turned them into shoe heels.

"With the money I made from the sale of my films, I bought the toy booth, where I've been trapped ever since, listening to the sounds of shoe heels clicking against the floor . . . the sound of my films disappearing forever into the dust. I was haunted by those ghosts for so many years. The only thing I couldn't bring myself to destroy was the automaton, which I donated to the local museum. But they never put it on display, and then the museum *itself* burned. The only thing left was the extra key I had made for my wife as an anniversary present long ago, and even that disappeared eventually. I thought the automaton was gone forever, but I was wrong. Miraculously, it survived. Tell me . . . where is it now?"

"I have it, at the train station," said Hugo.

"What is it doing at the train station?"

"That's a very long story," said Hugo.

"Bring it to me."

"Yes, sir. . . ." Hugo said. "I'll be right back."

9

The Ghost in the Station

HUGO PUT ON HIS SHOES and raced through the rain back to the train station, which was still crowded with travelers. He had no idea how he was going to manage it, but he couldn't wait to bring the automaton to Georges Méliès. He shook himself dry like a dog and sprinted across the crowded halls, excitement coursing through his body. His hand was hurting, and he knew it was going to be hard to carry the automaton back to the old man, so he stopped at the café to get some more ice. Making sure no one was watching, he grabbed a handful, as well as another bottle of milk. The newspaper vendor was talking with the owner of the café.

". . . I don't believe it. Here? Are you sure this is true, Madame Emile?" said the newspaperman.

"Yes, Monsieur Frick!" she answered. "My friend cleans the police station, and she overhears a lot," said Madame Emile. "I saw her on my way to work this morning. She told me that the police found a body at the bottom of the Seine a few days ago."

Hugo wanted to leave, but there was something about the woman's tone that made him stay. He crouched by the side of the café. "No one knows about this yet, but they will!" continued Madame Emile. "The river was being dredged, and they found the body of a man down there. He'd been at the bottom of the river for a very long time. Years maybe. My friend said that last night they finally figured out who it was, and they were only able to identify him by the silver flask clinging to an inside pocket. It took them a while to clean it off and read the name inscribed on the bottom. Guess who it turned out to be?"

Hugo already knew the answer.

"Remember the drunken old Timekeeper of the station?" continued Madame Emile. "It was him! Dead for years!"

Hugo knew she was wrong about that. Uncle Claude could only have been dead for a few months, but he wasn't going to correct her.

"Oh, my," said Monsieur Frick, who was used to being the one who knew things first. "Well, I guess nobody seemed to miss him."

"But don't you see what this means?" Madame Emile said. "The clocks in the station should have stopped working when he drowned since no one was taking care of them . . . but they didn't. They kept running perfectly! The Timekeeper was resting comfortably at the bottom of the river. Obviously he didn't want to be bothered, and his ghost kept the clocks running. But then they went and disturbed him and haven't you noticed? The clocks are all breaking down! The station is haunted!"

At that moment, Hugo accidentally dropped the ice and the bottle of milk, which shattered loudly on the stone floor. As Madame Emile spun around and spotted him, she yelled, "My milk! So you're the one who's been stealing from me!"

Hugo ran into the crowds as quickly as he could and disappeared into the walls, his head still reeling from what he had just heard. Back in his room, he took a few minutes to catch his breath. Then, because he had to get back to Isabelle's house as quickly as possible, he moved all the boxes away from the automaton's hiding place. He dragged the machine into the room and walked around it a few times, trying to figure out the best way to lift it up with his injured hand. Finally, he made sure it was completely covered with the fabric so it would be protected from the rain, and then he leaned the mechanical man into the crook of his elbow. With his good hand he managed, with great difficulty, to lift it up. He yelped in pain and staggered toward the door, which, out of habit, he had closed behind him when he came in. He knew he would have to put down the mechanical man to open the door, and he was trying to figure out the least painful way to do that when there was a knock.

"Isabelle?" Hugo said.

With a great deal of force the door flew open, and for a moment all Hugo could see was green. The Station Inspector burst in like a hurricane, followed immediately by Madame Emile and Monsieur Frick. The Station Inspector grabbed Hugo by the arm. Hugo yelled out, and to his horror he dropped the mechanical man, which landed on the ground with an awful ringing crash.

"That's him!" yelled Madame Emile. "He's been stealing milk and croissants from me for months."

"I saw the whole thing," cried Monsieur Frick. "He's a thief!"

"Thank you both very much. I'm glad you were able to follow the boy. Now please, I'll take care of things from here."

"What is this place?" asked Monsieur Frick, looking around.

"It's the Timekeeper's apartment," said the Station Inspector.

"The Timekeeper?" shrieked Madame Emile. Turning white as ghosts, she and Monsieur Frick ran from the doorway of Hugo's room.

The Station Inspector rolled his eyes and now focused his attention on Hugo, who was writhing in his arms. "Stay still!" he shouted, but his face changed immediately from anger to confusion when he looked down at the bundle lying on the floor. "What is going on in here? What is that?"

Other details about the Station Inspector, things that Hugo had never noticed before, came into focus. The man had bad teeth. The top part of one of his ears was missing. He smelled slightly of cabbages.

The Station Inspector, not letting go of Hugo, leaned over and moved the fabric until he could see the mechanical man lying on its side, its neck bent backward. "What in the world . . . ?" he said.

The Station Inspector walked around the room,

dragging Hugo after him, poking his head into doors and cabinets. At last he came to the pile of Uncle Claude's unopened paychecks. "What has happened to the Timekeeper? How did you know about his apartment here in the station and the tunnels in the walls? Where is he?"

"Please! My fingers are broken, grab my other arm — it hurts too much!" Hugo cried.

The Station Inspector saw the bandages and loosened his grip, at which point, like a wild animal, Hugo escaped.

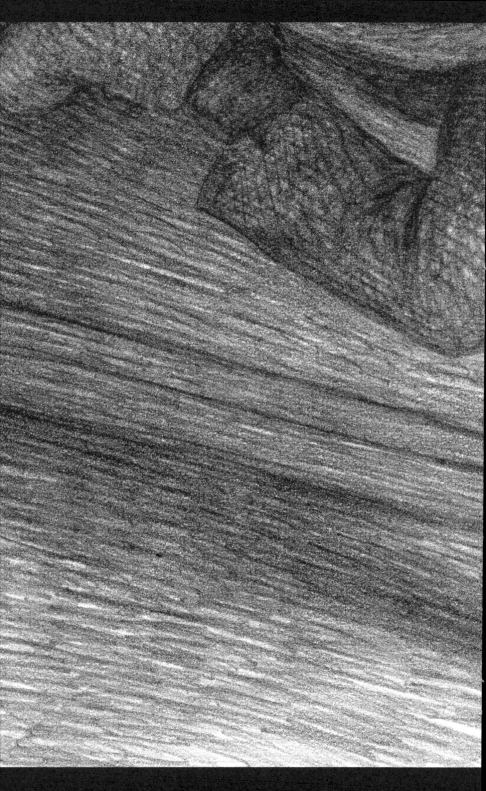

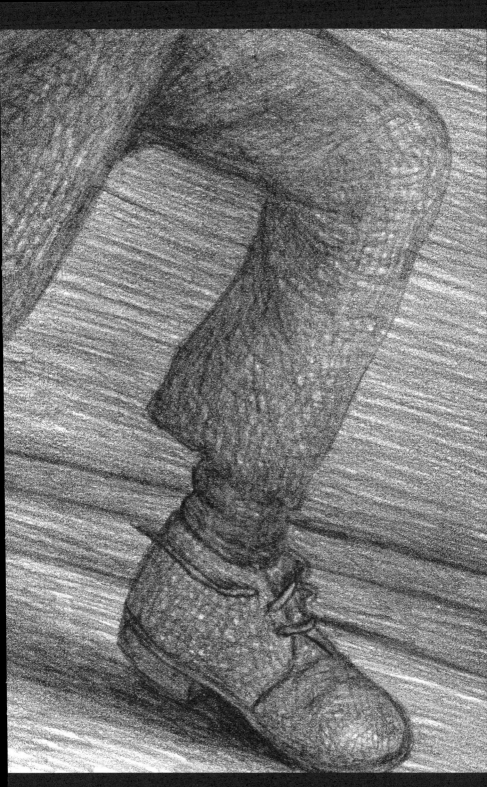

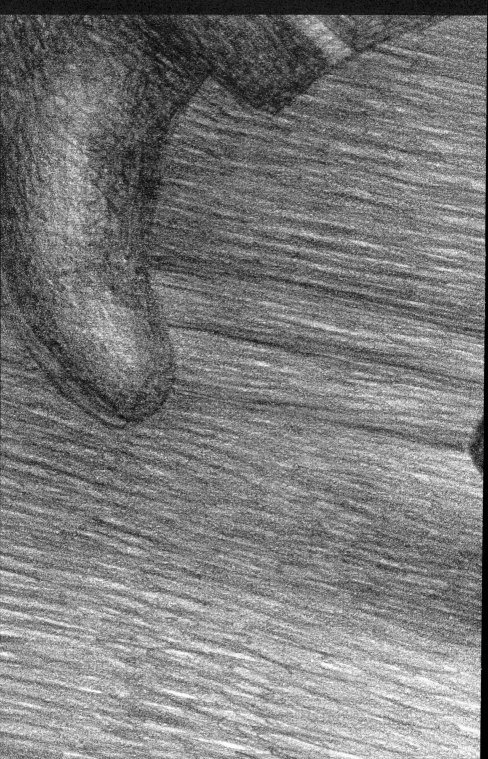

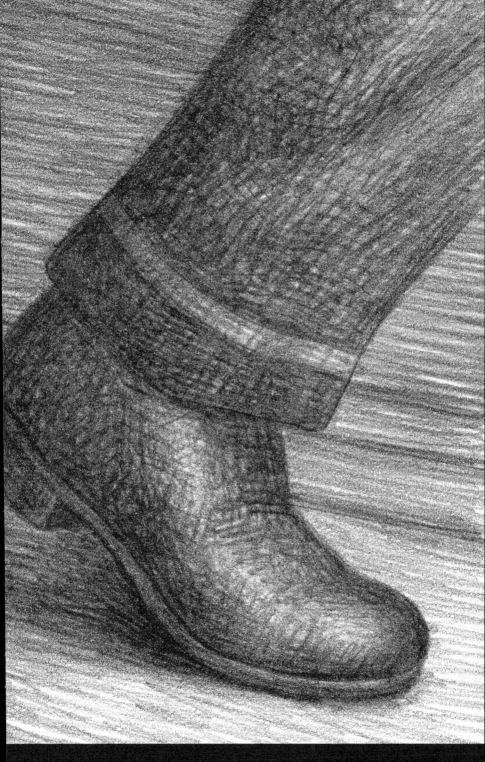

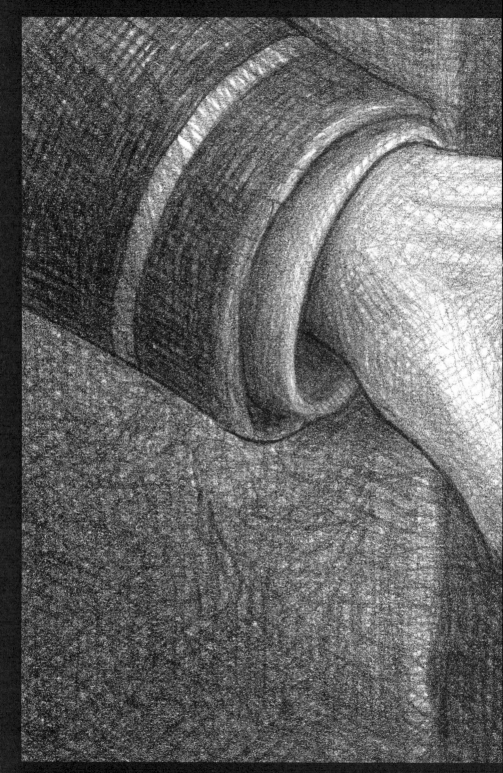

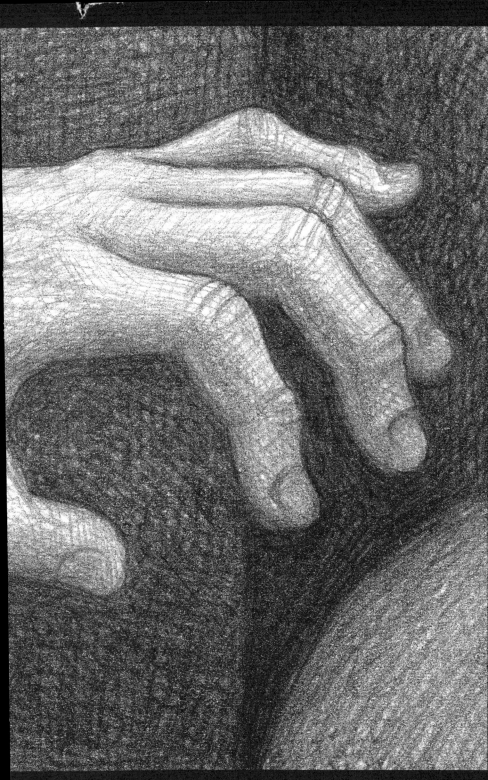

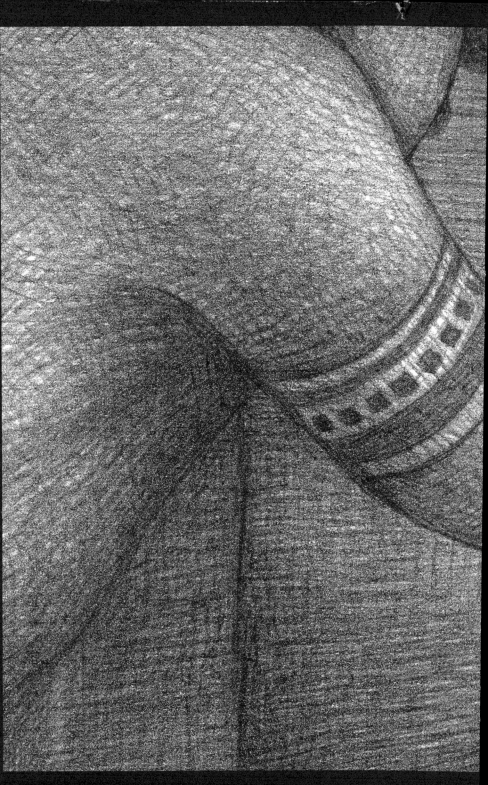

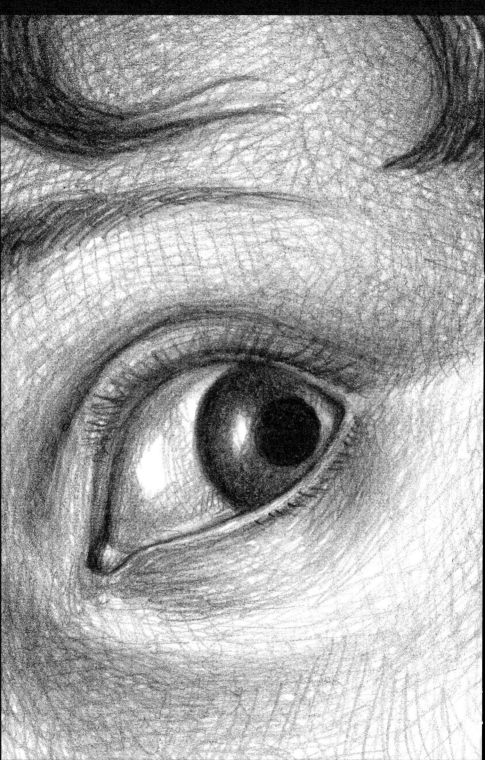

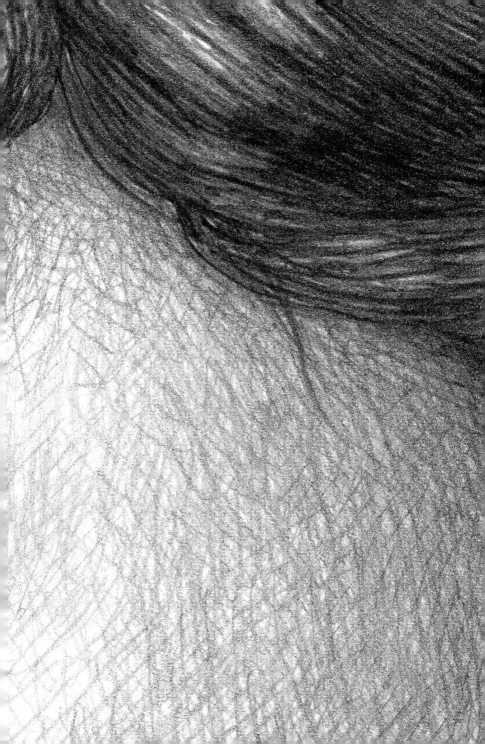

Crash!

Hugo smashed into someone's back, fell to the floor, looked up, and saw the hand of the Station Inspector as it closed in on him. He tried to roll the other way, but he found himself stopped by Madame Emile and Monsieur Frick, who descended on him through the crowd like vultures. They grabbed Hugo roughly and dragged him to his feet.

"Let me go!" cried Hugo. Hot tears welled in his eyes.

The Station Inspector leaned in close to Hugo's face as the café owner and the newspaperman held tightly to each arm. "The only place you're going is to prison!" the Station Inspector hissed.

10

A Train Arrives in the Station

"WHAT SHOULD WE DO WITH HIM?" asked Monsieur Frick.

"Follow me," said the Station Inspector, who led them back to his office. He opened the metal cell in the corner, and they threw Hugo inside. Then he quickly locked the cage, which Hugo had always feared so much, and tucked the key back into his pocket. The Station Inspector turned to Madame Emile and Monsieur Frick. "I promise you both he won't escape this time. I'll call the police, and you'll never be bothered by this slippery rat again."

The Station Inspector smiled when he said this, but it wasn't a friendly smile. It was a mean and dangerous smile. Madame Emile and Monsieur Frick bid farewell to the Station Inspector, leaving him alone with Hugo. The

Station Inspector called the police station, then said to Hugo, "Are you sure you don't want to confess now? No? Well then, I'll be back with a few of my friends. Don't go anywhere while I'm away." The Station Inspector laughed as he left the office and closed the door behind him.

Hugo sat there like an animal, wet and shivering in the corner of his cage. He wished Isabelle were here with one of her bobby pins.

Hugo was left by himself for a long time. He was going to be put in prison now, or an orphanage, he was sure of it. The mechanical man would be thrown away. He would never see Isabelle or her godparents again. He covered his eyes with his hands. Finally, the door to the office opened, and in came the Station Inspector with two policemen. Hugo stood up and tried to back himself farther into the corner of the tiny cage.

"He won't talk?" said one of the policemen.

"Nothing," said the Station Inspector.

"Well, maybe a ride to the police station will help out a little. Come on, boy. Your limousine is waiting." The Station Inspector opened the cage, and Hugo saw his opportunity. Once again he made a dash for it. He slipped between the police officers and ran back into the station.

It was crowded today, and Hugo was bounced from person to person as they shuffled through the station. By the time he came into a clearing, he had lost his sense of direction. He turned and saw the Station Inspector coming closer, with the two policemen right behind him. Hugo thought he saw Madame Emile and Monsieur Frick closing in quickly, too.

He kept running and was knocked over by some travelers rushing to catch their train. He landed on his hand and screamed in pain. He managed to get back up, and then, with tears blurring his vision and desperately trying to reach the front doors of the station, he stumbled and ran in exactly the wrong direction. He tripped and fell, several feet down, onto the tracks. He looked up, into the face of a train barreling into the station. From somewhere behind him he thought he heard a scream.

The horrible sound of the brakes being pulled, coupled with the metallic screech of the wheels against the rails, made it seem like the whole station was about to collapse around him. The black engine was zooming right toward Hugo and he was caught, unable to look away, as though he were watching a movie.

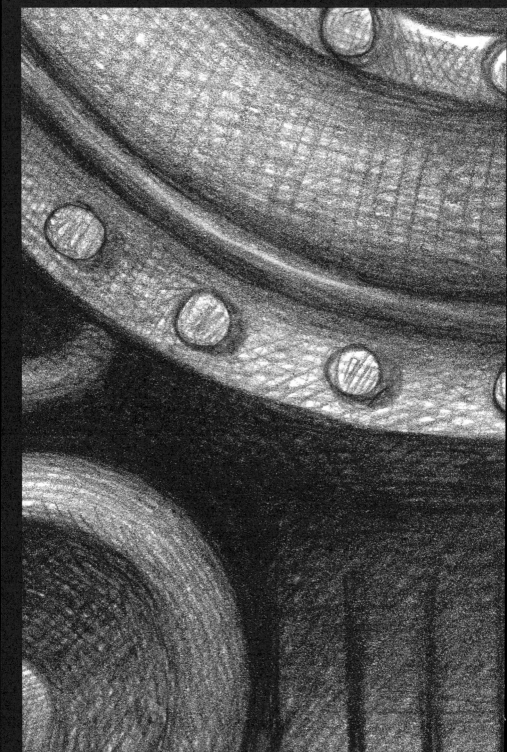

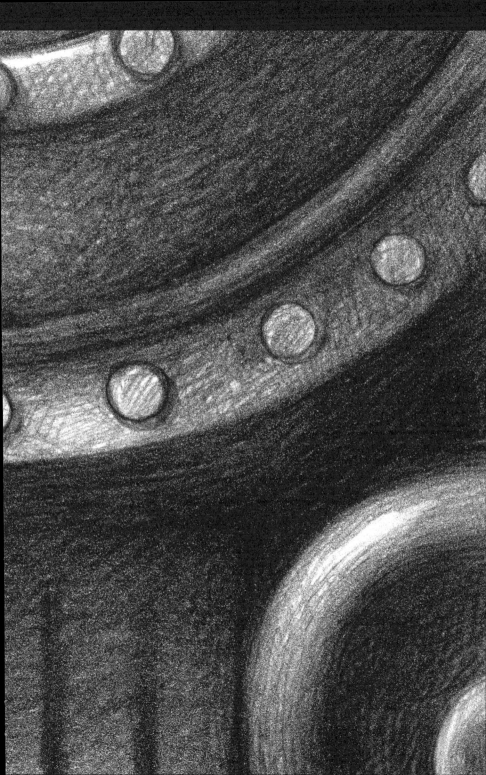

At the last possible moment, Hugo was yanked up, off the tracks, to safety. Smoke billowed out of the slowing engine as a shower of sparks flew from every wheel. Hugo felt dizzy.

There were a few moments of dazed silence, then steam was released from somewhere, and it made a sound like the train was sighing. For everyone on the train, nothing extraordinary had happened. They had simply pulled into the station. But for Hugo, his entire world was ending.

Again the Station Inspector was holding his arm, his injured hand throbbing with pain. He could see the policemen removing handcuffs from their belts, and finally the pain and the terror grew too much.

When Hugo opened his eyes, all he could see were stars. Stars and moons and what looked like a rocket ship. It was the cape from *A Trip to the Moon*, and Georges Méliès was wearing it.

"Ah, welcome back, Hugo Cabret," he said, holding the boy's head in his lap on a bench in the Station Inspector's office. Standing behind Hugo was Isabelle, leaning on her crutches. "Drink this," she said as she handed him a cup of water. "I knew something was wrong," she continued. "It was taking you much too long to come back home. Papa Georges insisted on coming with me. . . ."

The Station Inspector reached forward for Hugo, but the old man said, in his most dramatic voice, "Take your hands off of him."

"I'm sorry, sir. But as I was saying earlier, this boy was caught stealing from the café and from the Timekeeper, who has disappeared mysteriously. We believe he might be involved!"

Hugo saw that Madame Emile and Monsieur Frick had made their way into the office and were listening to everything.

"Tell him what you know, Hugo," said Georges Méliès.

Hugo gazed up into his eyes, which looked more

gentle and welcoming than he had ever seen before.

He whispered, "It's fine, Hugo. You're coming home with us. Now tell the Station Inspector what you know."

Hugo looked up at the Station Inspector. "The Timekeeper was my uncle, and I was his apprentice, but he drank, and he disappeared a while back, and I had to steal milk and croissants because I was hungry, and I've been taking care of the clocks ever since, and now he's dead and it will be in the papers tomorrow."

The Station Inspector studied Hugo, his eyebrows scowling. After what felt like an eternity, he unexpectedly started to laugh. The two policemen standing behind him looked confused.

"You?" said the Station Inspector. "You've been keeping the clocks running in this entire station? By yourself? A boy of ten! Ha!"

"I'm twelve," said Hugo.

The Station Inspector continued to laugh. "Well, old man, your little friend has quite a good imagination. Don't you think we would know if the Timekeeper was dead?"

"He is dead," said Madame Emile. "The boy is telling the truth."

"I'll vouch for that," said Monsieur Frick.

"But what was that . . . thing . . . you were stealing in the Timekeeper's apartment?"

"I wasn't stealing it," said Hugo, who looked up at the old man and said, "I dropped it! It's broken again."

"I'm not worried about that. I think between the two of us we can have it fixed up pretty quickly." Georges Méliès turned to the Station Inspector. "You can't steal something that you already own, now, can you? That machine is his. We'll figure out how to repay you, madame, for the milk and the croissants. But now I think it's time for us to get out of this station."

He helped Hugo stand. The children were enveloped by the soft folds of the old man's cape, and together they all headed home.

SIX MONTHS LATER

ONTHS
ER

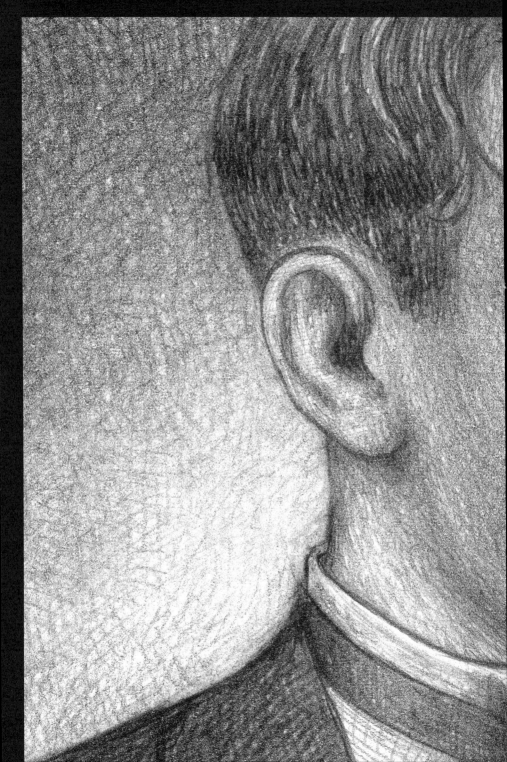

11

The Magician

HUGO FINISHED PUTTING ON HIS TUXEDO. He rubbed the buttons and admired how smooth and shiny they were. Catching his reflection in the mirror, he stared for a moment. He thought that he looked almost grown-up.

The Mélièses had emptied out a small storage room in the back of their apartment, and now that room belonged to Hugo. The French Film Academy, through the intervention of René Tabard, arranged for money to be given to the Méliès family, and some of that money went into furnishing Hugo's room. There was a small workbench at one end, and it was covered in little mechanical creatures made out of clockworks, and magic tricks of all shapes and sizes, which Hugo had made himself. The school year had begun again, and Hugo had a desk for doing homework. His shelves were covered in books, and he had many souvenirs from the Paris World's Fair, which he and Isabelle had attended a month earlier. His father's notebook was safe inside a box in his bedside table. His floor was littered with drawings. He had a little drawer just for the ticket stubs of the movies he and Isabelle saw together.

In the darkness of a new cinema that opened in a nearby neighborhood, Hugo was able to travel backward through time and see dinosaurs and pirates and cowboys, and he saw the future, with robots and cities so gigantic they blocked out the sky. He flew in airplanes and crossed the ocean in ships. In the dark of the movie theater he first saw jungles, oceans, and deserts. He wanted to visit them all in real life.

In one corner of the room stood the automaton, which Hugo and Papa Georges had repaired to perfection.

Hugo stuffed his pockets with little magic tricks and cards as he usually did, checked his railroad watch, and knocked on Isabelle's door. She opened the door wearing a white dress that seemed to glow.

In the living room, Georges Méliès had on a tuxedo with his black celestial cape (which had been lovingly mended and cleaned by his wife and was now as bright and colorful as the day it was made), and she wore a dress that sparkled like water. Etienne soon arrived, wearing a beautiful black tuxedo and a brand-new eye patch.

Hugo picked up the invitation that lay on the table.

The French Film Academy
Invites you to join us
For an evening celebrating the life and work
Of cinema legend
G E O R G E S   M É L I È S

Two gleaming motorcars pulled up to the doors of their apartment building and everyone headed outside.

"Oh! My camera!" said Isabelle. "I almost forgot." She raced back to her room and got the black-and-silver camera her godparents had given her for her birthday.

"Will you carry some extra film for me tonight?" she asked Hugo as she handed him the rolls, which he stuffed into his pocket. "And I've been meaning to give this to you." She then handed Hugo a photo she had taken of him with his old friends Antoine and Louis. They all had their arms around one another's necks and they were laughing.

"Thanks," said Hugo. He smiled and slipped it into his jacket pocket.

Isabelle adjusted the camera and the key on its chain around her neck so they hung properly.

Outside, the drivers helped them into the cars, and off they sped to the Film Academy.

"It's been a very long time since I've been here," said the old man as they neared their destination. "Maybe I'll ask to see the picture of Prometheus I painted when I was young."

"You painted that picture, Papa Georges?" said Hugo, amazed. "I *thought* it was of Prometheus. I saw it in the library."

"It's still hanging? That's good news. You know the myth, then?"

The children told him they did.

"Then you know Prometheus was rescued in the end. His chains were broken, and he was finally set free." The old man squinted one of his eyes and added, "How about that?"

Once everyone was seated in the theater, Monsieur

Tabard went to the podium. "Good evening, ladies and gentlemen," he said. "My name is René Tabard, and I will be your host for this evening. We have gathered here tonight to honor one of our pioneers, Georges Méliès, who brought magic to the movies. For years, his films were believed to be lost. Indeed, Monsieur Méliès himself was believed to be gone. But we have a most wonderful surprise for the world. Monsieur Méliès is here tonight, and not all of his films were destroyed. Thanks to the diligence of one of the students here, Etienne Pruchon, and with help on the weekends from Hugo and Isabelle, the two brave children who are being raised by Monsieur and Madame Méliès, we went back and checked one last time. Starting with one film that we found in our own basement, Etienne, Hugo, and Isabelle searched through vaults and long-closed archives. They took trips to private collections and such strange places as barns and catacombs, where their work was richly rewarded. They found old negatives, boxes of prints, and trunks full of decaying film, which we were able to save. We now have in our possession over eighty films by Monsieur Méliès. A small fraction of the five hundred he produced, but I'm confident that in the years to come even more of his movies will resurface.

"Tonight, Georges Méliès, my boyhood hero, is

being rediscovered. Now sit back, open your eyes, and be prepared to dream. Ladies and gentlemen, I present to you the world of Georges Méliès."

The audience cheered and applauded.

The lights went down and the orchestra began to play as the curtains opened. Film by film, Georges' world was projected on screen for the first time in over a decade.

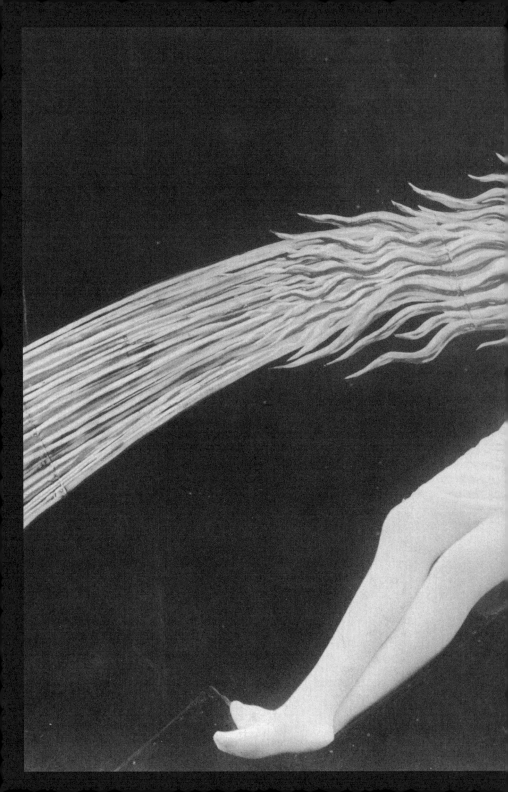

And then, the last film shown was *A Trip to the Moon.*

Hugo looked at Isabelle. Tears were running down her cheeks in two thin, glimmering lines.

The lights came up and the man of honor was then invited up on stage, where he was given a gold laurel wreath to wear as a crown. He stepped to the podium and said to the audience in a proud, emotion-filled voice, "As I look out at all of you gathered here, I want to say that I don't see a room full of Parisians in top hats and diamonds and silk dresses. I don't see bankers and housewives and store clerks. No. I address you all tonight as you truly are: wizards, mermaids, travelers, adventurers, and magicians. You are the true dreamers."

After the gala ended, they all went to a small party in his honor at a nearby restaurant. Isabelle took photographs the entire night, and Hugo sat at a table doing magic tricks.

A rather sizable crowd soon gathered around Hugo.

Georges Méliès walked over to where Hugo was sitting, put his hand on Hugo's shoulder, and said to everyone, "I want you all to remember this moment. I believe this is the first public performance ever given by Professor Alcofrisbas."

Hugo looked up and asked, "Who is Professor Alcofrisbas?"

"You are, my boy! Professor Alcofrisbas was a character who appeared in many of my films, sometimes as an explorer, sometimes as an alchemist — a person who can turn anything to gold. But, mostly, he was a magician, and now he has appeared in real life, right here, in this very room."

In that moment, the machinery of the world lined up. Somewhere a clock struck midnight, and Hugo's future seemed to fall perfectly into place.

12

Winding It Up

TIME CAN PLAY ALL SORTS OF TRICKS ON YOU.

In the blink of an eye, babies appear in carriages, coffins disappear into the ground, wars are won and lost, and children transform, like butterflies, into adults.

That's what happened to me.

Once upon a time, I was a boy named Hugo Cabret, and I desperately believed that a broken automaton would save my life. Now that my cocoon has fallen away and I have emerged as a magician named Professor Alcofrisbas, I can look back and see that I was right.

The automaton my father discovered *did* save me.

But now I have built a new automaton.

I spent countless hours designing it. I made every gear myself, carefully cut every brass disk, and fashioned every last bit of machinery with my own hands.

When you wind it up, it can do something I'm sure no other automaton in the world can do. It can tell you the incredible story of Georges Méliès, his wife, their goddaughter, and a beloved clock maker whose son grew up to be a magician.

The complicated machinery inside my automaton can produce one hundred and fifty-eight different pictures, and it can write, letter by letter, an entire book, twenty-six thousand one hundred and fifty-nine words.

These words.

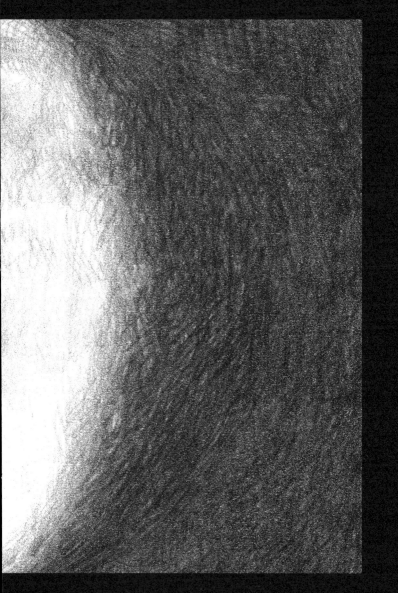

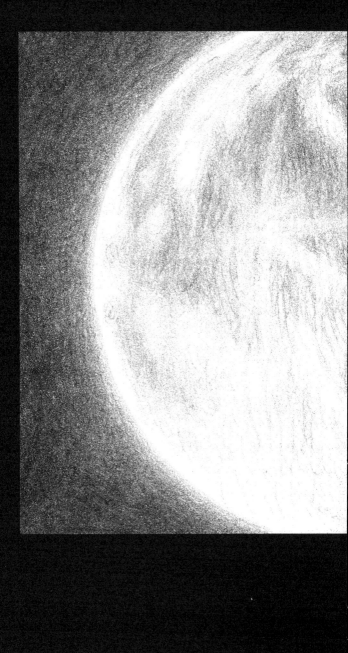

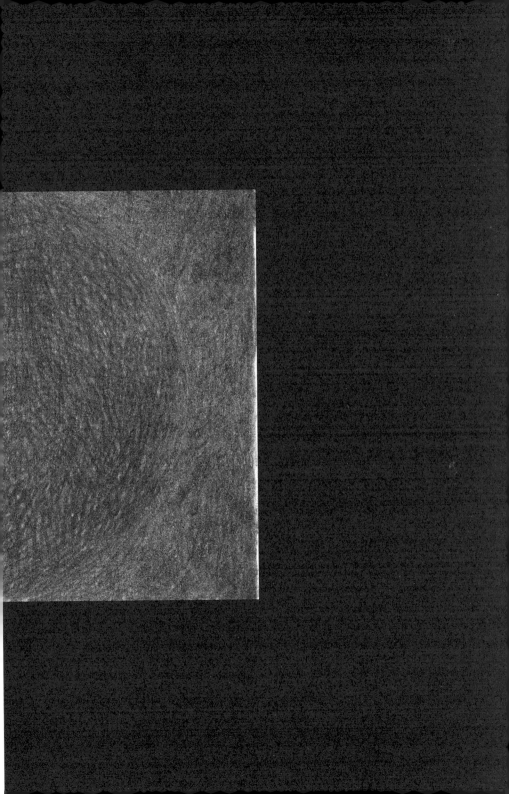

THE

END

Acknowledgements

I HAD LONG WANTED TO WRITE a story about Georges Méliès, but it wasn't until I read a book called *Edison's Eve: A Magical History of the Quest for Mechanical Life* by Gaby Wood that this story began to really take shape. The book discussed Méliès' collection of automata, which was donated to a museum, where it was neglected in a damp attic and eventually thrown away. I imagined a boy finding those machines in the garbage, and at that moment, Hugo and this story were born.

I would like to thank Charles Penniman, who spent

an afternoon with me in the basement of the Franklin Institute in Philadelphia, showing me the workings of a nineteenth-century automaton. The automaton came to the museum in 1928, after being damaged in a fire. It had stopped working, but once it was refurbished, it surprised its new owners by drawing four different pictures and writing three different poems. And, like the fictional story I had already made up of Hugo fixing the automaton and finding out it was made by Georges Méliès because it signs his name, the automaton at the Franklin Institute, once it was fixed, signed the name of its maker, Maillardet, thus solving the mystery of its provenance.

To see the Maillardet automaton and learn more about it, you can go to http://www.fi.edu/pieces/knox/automaton/

Thanks also to Senior Curator John Alviti for arranging this visit at the Franklin Institute for me.

I want to thank Lisa Holton, Ellie Berger, Andrea Pinkney, and everyone at Scholastic for all their support and encouragement. I want to thank David Saylor and Charles Kreloff for their beautiful design work on this book, and Abby Ranger and Lillie Mear for all their assistance in bringing everything together.

And I'm eternally grateful to Tracy Mack and Leslie Budnick, who worked tirelessly with me on *The Invention of Hugo Cabret.* Over the course of nearly two years they helped me sand, file, build, refine, and polish it. I don't have enough words to express my gratitude. This book truly wouldn't exist without them.

Huge thanks to Tanya Blumstein, my Parisian connection, for all of the introductions, e-mails, translations, advice, and all-around French know-how. She was invaluable during the making of this book. I'd also like to acknowledge all the translations and phone calls that were made on my behalf by Etienne Pelaprat, whose first name made its way into the book.

Thanks to film historian Glenn Myrent, whom Tanya introduced me to. Glenn helped me in Paris and answered many questions for me about early French cinema.

I also extend my appreciation to Andy Baron, mechanical genius, who spent hours with me on the phone going over the technical aspects of clocks, automata, gears, pulleys, mechanisms, and motors. Andy told me he saw a little of himself in Hugo, and I'm sure Hugo would be flattered to hear that.

The following scholars helped me with the early history of French film: Melinda Barlow, Associate Professor of Film Studies, University of Colorado at Boulder; Claudia Gorbman, Professor of Film Studies, Interdisciplinary Arts and Sciences Program, University of Washington, Tacoma; and Professor Tom Gunning, Committee on Cinema and Media, University of Chicago. I thank them for advising me on movies to see and what films Hugo and Isabelle would have enjoyed, as well as helping me understand the world of Georges Méliès and his incredible vision.

My appreciation also goes to Sebastian Laws of the Sutton Clock Shop, who let me look around his shop (which was founded by his father), answered questions, and allowed me to take pictures.

And thanks to the following friends and colleagues for their advice, input, time, translations, and feedback on this story: Lisa Cartwright, Deborah de Furia, Cara Falcetti, David Levithan, Peter Mendelsund, Billy Merrell, Linda Sue Park, Susan Raboy, Pam Muñoz Ryan, Noel Silverman, Alexander Stadler, Danielle Tcholakian, Sarah Weeks, and Jonah Zuckerman.

And finally, thanks of course to David Serlin, for everything.

Credits

Fairies), 1903

Pages 292-293, drawing of a fire-breathing bird

Pages 294-295, drawing based on *La Chrysalide et le papillon d'or (The Brahmin and the Butterfly)*, 1901

Pages 296-297, drawing of a cave with bats (sketch for a set design)

From the collection of the British Film Institute:

Pages 352-353, still from *Le Voyage dans la lune (A Trip to the Moon)*, 1902

Pages 356-359, two stills from *Escamotage d'une dame au théâtre Robert Houdin (Vanishing Lady)*, 1896

Pages 498-499, still from *Deux cent mille lieues sous les mers (20,000 Leagues Under the Sea)*, 1906

Pages 500-501, still from *Rêve de Noël (Christmas Dream)*, 1900

Pages 502-503, still from *L'éclipse du soleil en pleine lune (The Eclipse)*, 1907

Pages 504-505, still from *Les quatre cents farces du diable (The Merry Frolics of Satan)*, 1906

Please note that the drawings on pages 252-253 and 388-389 are copyright © 2007 by Brian Selznick, inspired by works by Georges Méliès.

THE FILMS MENTIONED IN THIS BOOK ALL EXIST:

L'Arrivée d'un train à la Ciotat (The Arrival of a Train at La Ciotat), 1895, the Lumière brothers (When Hugo reads about this film, it is referred to as *A Train Arrives in the Station.*)

Le Voyage dans la lune (A Trip to the Moon), 1902, Georges Méliès

Escamotage d'une dame au théâtre Robert Houdin (Vanishing Lady), 1896, Georges Méliès

Safety Last, 1923, Harold Lloyd

A Clock Store, 1931, A Walt Disney Silly Symphony cartoon

Paris qui dort (Paris Asleep), 1924, René Clair (This is the movie about stopping time that Hugo refers to in the clock tower with Isabelle.)
Le million (The Million), 1931, René Clair

SOME FILMS BY THE OTHER DIRECTORS MENTIONED IN THIS STORY:
The Kid, 1921, Charlie Chaplin
Sherlock Jr., 1924, Buster Keaton
The Little Match Girl, 1928, Jean Renoir

AND THREE FILMS THAT WERE VERY INFLUENTIAL IN THE CREATION OF THIS STORY:
Zéro de conduite (Zero for Conduct), 1933, Jean Vigo
Les quatre cents coups (The 400 Blows), 1959, François Truffaut
Sous les toits de Paris (Under the Roofs of Paris), 1930, René Clair

THIS IS A WORK OF FICTION.
While Georges Méliès was a real filmmaker, I have completely imagined his personality.

To find out about the real Georges Méliès, check out the following Web site and then go to the library:
http://www.missinglinkclassichorror.co.uk/index.htm (Type "Méliès" into the search engine in this site, and you'll find very good links to his life story.)

A recent book for children about early cinema has a good chapter about the working career of Georges Méliès. The book, Paul Clee's *Before Hollywood: From Shadow Play to the Silver Screen*, is published by Clarion Books.

And while Georges Méliès actually existed, Hugo and Isabelle are entirely my own invention.

The text of this book was set in 12-point
Monotype Bulmer. Named after the English printer William Bulmer
(1757-1830), this typeface was redrawn and digitized by
Monotype based on designs created in 1928 by Morris Fuller Benton, which
were in turn based on the original typefaces designed by William
Martin in 1792 for Bulmer's press.

The display type was set in P22 Parrish Roman, designed in
1999 by Richard Kegler for the P22 type foundry.
The Parrish letterforms were inspired by the hand-drawn lettering
of American artist Maxfield Parrish (1870-1966).

This book was printed on 80# Finch Opaque
Vellum paper and has been thread-sewn in 16-page signatures
and bound by RR Donnelley in Crawfordsville, Indiana.

Brian Selznick's drawings for this book were created in
pencil on Fabriano Artistico watercolor paper.